CHLOE IN THE KNOW

"Chloe?" said her mother, opening the door a crack. "Can I come in?"

"I guess," said Chloe, wishing she could say no.

Her mother entered the room. "Why is it so dark in here?" she said. "Is something the matter?" Mrs. Kane perched on the edge of the bed.

Chloe shrugged her shoulders.

"Grandma loved the poem you wrote. She couldn't stop talking about it."

"It wasn't so great," said Chloe.

"I thought it was wonderful."

"You only love me if I do wonderful things," said Chloe.

Chloe's mother looked hurt. "That's not true," she said. "I love you because...well, you're not Harry and you're not Dorothy—you're you."

"I'm a liar," said Chloe. "I didn't write that card."

CHLOE IN THE KNOW

A Beech Tree Paperback Book
New York

The Library of Congress has cataloged the Greenwillow Books
edition of *Chloe in the Know* as follows:

Caseley, Judith
    Chloe in the know / by Judith Caseley,
        p.   cm.
    Summary: Chloe's close and caring family supports her
when she begins to feel the strain of being the oldest child
    ISBN 0-688-11055-X
    [1. Family Life—Fiction.
2. Brothers and sisters—Fiction.]
I. Title
[PZ7.C2677Ch   1993]
[Fic]—dc20
92-14757   CIP   AC

First Beech Tree Edition, 1994.
ISBN 0-688-013069-0

For SCH,
with love again

and special thanks
to Irene Chin

Contents

1 ○ Chloe's Nose   1

2 ○ Chloe's Card   23

3 ○ Mrs. Kane's Tummy Ache   41

4 ○ Chloe in the Know   54

5 ○ Chloe's Class Trip   73

6 ○ Chloe's Fortune   93

7 ○ Mickey   115

1

Chloe's Nose

CHLOE KANE couldn't understand why one day she thought she was pretty, with her long straight hair and deep brown eyes, and the next day she thought she was uglier than the Wicked Witch of the West in *The Wizard of Oz.*

Chloe looked in the mirror and made a face. "I look terrible," she said out loud.

Her brother Harry, who was playing Ken and Barbie dolls with his two sisters, held Ken in front of his face so that it looked like Ken was talking. "No, you don't," said Harry, in his deepest voice. "Your eyes are just like Mr. Ritter's cocker spaniel's."

1

"Thanks a lot," said Chloe sarcastically, even though she knew it was supposed to be a compliment, because Mr. Ritter's cocker spaniel had beautiful eyes.

"You're welcome," said Harry and Ken.

Chloe held out a lock of her long brown hair and let it go. It fell straight down and lay there, without a hint of a curl. "Why don't I have hair like my new Barbie?" she said, holding the blond-haired, curly-headed doll up to her face.

"I like brown hair the best," said Dorothy, who had brown hair herself.

"So do I," said Mr. Kane from behind his newspaper.

Chloe refused to feel better. She took one finger and pushed at her nose so that it would turn up at the end like her brother's. It wasn't fair. Her nose was slightly hooked, just like her father's.

"You have a Roman nose," Mr. Kane told her when she complained. "Everybody wants a Roman nose. It's aquiline."

"How could I have a Roman nose?" said

2

Chloe grumpily, turning her head first one way and then the other. "We're not from Rome."

"Rome is in Italy," said Dorothy, smearing Hello Kitty lipstick on her mouth, because it wasn't a school day and makeup was only allowed on the weekends. "Gina Greco's mother showed us how to make lasagna at school, and Gina's grandma was born in Rome, and that's in Italy." Dorothy pursed her lips. "Does my lipstick look like Barbie's lipstick?"

"It's nice," said Mr. Kane, "but a little heavy."

"I'm a movie star," said Dorothy, starting on her rouge.

"With a movie star's nose," said Chloe. "You're so lucky. I've got a Roman nose, and we're not even from Italy."

"Grandma Rebecca is from Russia," said Harry, jumping on his father's lap. "So you have a Russian nose. An aqua Russian nose."

"Not aqua," said Dorothy. "That's a color."

"A Russian nose would be red," said Harry, "from the cold. Mrs. Eisen says that Russia is freezing. She showed us pictures."

"It is cold in Russia," said Mr. Kane, "but the word is aquiline."

Harry jumped off his father's lap and pulled a fat red book off the shelf. "How do you spell it?" he said, turning the pages.

Chloe grabbed the dictionary from her brother. "First graders can hardly read," said Chloe.

"*E, A, T,*" said Harry. "Eat. I can spell. *P, U.* You smell."

Chloe ignored him and thumbed through the pages. "Is it spelled *A, K?*" she said to her father.

"*A, Q,*" said Mr. Kane. He pulled Harry onto his lap again. "Your fingernails are like claws, young man," he said, taking the nail scissors and snipping away at Harry's left pinky nail.

"I've found it!" said Chloe, bending over the page to read. Her mouth fell open, and she slammed the book shut.

"Read it," said Dorothy, putting down her eye-shadow brush.

"It's awful," said Chloe. She was combing her straight hair so hard that it looked like it hurt.

4

Dorothy found the page and read out loud: "'Aquiline. Like an eagle's beak. Curved or hooked.'" She closed the book quietly, screwed up her nose, and looked accusingly at her father. "Chloe doesn't look like an eagle," she said.

"She has a beautiful nose!" said Mr. Kane, scissors in the air as he started on Harry's other hand. "It's just like mine!"

"We saw an eagle at school," said Harry. "His name was King, and he could pluck chickens and eat mice."

"I don't eat mice," said Chloe glumly.

Harry slipped off his father's lap and stood next to Chloe. "I used to look like King," he said sadly.

"You did not," said Chloe.

Harry held out his fingers and wriggled them. "I used to have claws," he said. "Before Daddy cut them off."

"That's talons," said Chloe. "Eagles have talons. We learned that in science."

"Chloe, you know what?" Harry looked very serious now.

5

"What?" Chloe combed her hair behind her ears. Maybe a ponytail would be an improvement.

"You're a lot like an eagle," said Harry.

"Harry Kane!" said his father. "Enough!"

"She is!" said Harry. "Chloe is smart. And eagles are the smartest birds in the world."

"Thanks," said Chloe, fastening a red bow around her ponytail. She swung her head around to face her father and brother and sister. "What do you think?" she said.

Harry took a long look. "You remind me of something," he said.

Dorothy put her hands on her hips and said, "Hmm."

Mr. Kane smiled and said, "You look gorgeous!"

"I know!" said Harry. "An elf! You look like the elf on my cereal box!"

"Why does she look like an elf?" said Dorothy.

"Because her ears stick out," said Harry.

Chloe was smart, but she didn't have very

good aim, because the hairbrush she threw at Harry missed him by a mile.

Harry was right about Chloe being smart. She had been smart even as a baby, though she didn't say a single word for the first two years of her life. Grandma Rebecca had said that maybe she needed a speech teacher. Mr. Kane had said you could see the intelligence in her eyes. Mrs. Kane had agreed, but couldn't help noticing that the other children in the playground said "botty" if they wanted their bottle, and "cookie" if they were hungry, and "dada!" if their fathers arrived. Chloe just pointed or said "uh!"

A few days after her second birthday, Chloe pointed to the lamp on the table next to her and said, "Light bulb." Then she went through the rest of the house naming the furniture and her stuffed animals and people in photographs and the television set and even Bert and Ernie and Oscar the Grouch. Her mother was so amazed that she called Mr. Kane at the post office where he worked.

When Mr. Kane walked in the door, Chloe ran and threw her arms around him and said, "Daddy!"

"To think that her very first words were 'light bulb'!" said Mrs. Kane.

Mr. Kane shook his head. "I told you I could see the intelligence in her eyes," he said. "A light bulb went on in her head!"

Chloe's mother and father laughed, and it became a family story. "Light bulb" were Chloe's first words, and "Mama" was Dorothy's, and Harry said "ice cream" quite clearly when he was only thirteen months old.

But being smart just wasn't enough. When Chloe went to school on Monday, she thought her red polka-dot dress made her look a little like a ballerina. But she still had the same plain old straight brown hair and aquiline nose.

Chloe sat next to her best friend Mei-Hua in class and behind Theresa.

"That's the kind of hair I'd like," said Chloe, pointing to Theresa's curly blond hair.

"Not me," said Mei-Hua, shaking her short dark hair. "I like it this way."

"Yours is Chinese," said Chloe. "That's the way it grows."

"Yours isn't Chinese, and it's straight like mine."

"Dorothy's hair is wavy, and so is Grandma's. They lucked out."

While Mrs. Mellor started talking about how the immigrants settled in New York City, Chloe wrapped a strand of hair around her pencil and held it there. Maybe by the end of history it would curl.

Mrs. Mellor obviously didn't care if it curled, because she called on Chloe and said, "Take the pencil out of your hair, please. Did any members of your family leave their country and settle in a new country?"

"My Grandma Rebecca was from Russia," said Chloe. "She got a job sewing when she came over here." It was funny that her mother couldn't sew like Grandma. Mr. Kane did all the sewing in the family.

"And your grandfather?" Mrs. Mellor asked.

"Grandpa Leon owned a candy store," said Chloe. Chloe's mother got to eat lots of candy and ice cream when she was little. So how come she made Chloe and the rest of the family eat sunflower seeds and frozen yogurt most of the time?

"I'd like you to talk to your grandparents and record their immigrant experiences," said Mrs. Mellor. "Any of you who know someone who settled here from another country, ask them to tell you about it. What did it feel like to come to a strange country, with new customs and a language they didn't speak?"

Chloe heard Bucky say, "Hurray! I don't know anybody."

Theresa whispered, "I think mine are all dead!"

Mrs. Mellor continued. "For those of you who don't have anybody, I'd like you to imagine what it would be like and what it would feel like, and write it down."

Theresa thumped her fist on the desk. "Oh, boy," she said. "Too bad they're dead. Now I have to make it all up!"

Chloe giggled, but not too loudly, because Mrs. Mellor had a nickname—Mellor the Yeller—and she was pretty strict about noise.

After school, Chloe sat at the kitchen table while Mrs. Kane made dinner. She was stumped. Mrs. Mellor had given them two days to write the story, but she couldn't find any immigrants. Grandma and Grandpa were away at a hotel and Great-Grandma Fanny was in a nursing home. Aunt Sydelle lived in Florida and Mrs. Kane wouldn't let Chloe call her because it was long distance.

"Interview me," said Mrs. Kane, shaping minced turkey meat into patties.

"You're not an immigrant," said Chloe, but she got her pencil ready. "Do you remember what it was like?"

"I remember that my lunches were different from some of the other kids' lunches at school, and they made fun of me. Grandma didn't know about peanut butter and jelly, and she wrapped my food in old wrappers or scraps of paper that she didn't want to waste."

"How did you feel?" Chloe wrote down *different food.*

"I was embarrassed. But when Grandpa Leon

opened the candy store, they learned quickly."

"Grandma started using Baggies?"

Mrs. Kane laughed. "Probably waxed paper. And definitely no Ziplocs!"

Chloe wrote down *waxed paper*.

"I remember one time," said Mrs. Kane, shaking her head. "It was cold outside and my mother made me wear a babushka."

"What's a babushka?" Chloe didn't write anything down.

"It's a kerchief, a Russian kerchief, but none of the other kids wore one, and it made me look . . ." Mrs. Kane rinsed her hands in a basin of soapy water. "Foreign," she said, drying them.

"What do you mean, foreign?"

"Like a Russian peasant. Different. Not like the other kids. And I wanted so much to fit in. So, every day, I let my mother tie the babushka around my head, and I took it off as soon as I rounded the corner."

"You didn't want to hurt your mother's feelings?"

"No." Mrs. Kane smiled. "But she found out.

One day she ran after me because I'd forgotten my lunch, and she saw me take it off."

"Did she yell at you?"

"She never said a word. But I remember the next day, instead of rugelach for dessert, my mother had packed Mallomars. Just like the other kids got."

Chloe tried to picture herself walking to school with a babushka on her head. Children would laugh and point. She would feel alone and different.

At suppertime, Chloe ate a turkey burger and a baked potato. She ate two pieces of broccoli. She smiled when her mother gave her Mallomars for dessert. What would it feel like to unwrap a strange-looking cookie in front of her friends at school? She remembered that Harry had stopped bringing tofu hot dogs for lunch because Ivan Seeger said they were the grossest things he had ever seen, and everybody laughed.

After her bath, Chloe combed her wet hair. It lay there, flat and straight, mounding slightly only when it hit her elf ears.

Dorothy combed the back of it for her. "Lots of people would love to have hair like yours," she said.

"I'd give anything for curls like Theresa Sidoti," said Chloe.

"I'll set it for you," said Dorothy. "I've set Baby Curlylocks lots of times."

Chloe looked doubtful. "That's a doll," she said, but she didn't stop Dorothy from asking her mother for rollers.

"Are you sure you don't need any help?" said Mrs. Kane, pulling a bag out of the hall closet.

"No, thanks," said Dorothy. "I've seen Marie at the beauty parlor do it a million times, and I've practiced on Baby Curlylocks."

Dorothy gave Chloe the bag. "You hand me one of them at a time," she said.

"Try to make it look like this," said Chloe, taking her curly-haired blond Barbie doll off her dresser.

At last, Chloe's head was covered in rollers. They weren't very even, but Dorothy tied a large kerchief around them quite expertly. "You'll

14

have to sleep in them," she told Chloe, because Mr. Kane had warned them twice that it was time to go to bed.

Chloe woke up tired, with an aching head from the hard rollers. Dorothy pulled them out quickly while Chloe screeched.

"Baby Curlylocks never complained like you do," said Dorothy, brushing Chloe's hair hard. Dorothy stepped back. "Look at me," she said. She stood there, then brushed some more. She was silent.

Chloe looked in the mirror. She was a witch, with wild, frizzy, lumpy, bumpy hair. "Mommmmm!" she yelled, and Mrs. Kane came running.

"Oh, my heavens," she said when she saw Chloe.

"I'm washing it," said Chloe, but Mrs. Kane wouldn't let her because it was time to leave, and besides, it was cold outside.

Mrs. Kane took the brush from Dorothy and ran it through Chloe's hair. "There," she said. "It's a little better. Now get your coats on."

Walnut School was only a block away, but to Chloe it felt like a mile. There were hoots and hollers, and Harry's best friend Benjamin called her Bozo the Clown. Carl Spignolli said, "That's some crazy do!" and Harry, her very own brother Harry, said, "Doo doo!" and laughed his head off.

In the classroom, Mei-Hua told Chloe that her hairdo was kind of interesting, but Bucky added, "If you want your hair to look like a science project."

Mrs. Mellor became Mellor the Yeller and the class quieted down. When she started talking about the Great Depression of 1929, Chloe whispered to Mei-Hua, "I think I'm in it."

Mrs. Mellor gave her the evil eye, and Chloe raised her hand. "I have to go to the bathroom," she said in a small voice. Chloe raced out of the room and bent her head over the sink. She splashed some water onto her hair. Chloe looked in the mirror, and her heart sank. It was worse. Now one side of her hair was wet and straight and the other side was curly. She took some paper towels and rubbed her wet hair as dry as she could get it, so that Mrs. Mellor wouldn't become Mellor the Yeller again when she saw Chloe's wet hair.

"Get your gym shoes," said Mrs. Mellor when Chloe reappeared. She didn't say a word about her hair.

In gym class, Chloe hoped that her curly hair would turn straight from all the running, but it just flapped wildly and got in her eyes.

At lunchtime, she sat next to Mei-Hua and they traded sandwiches. Chloe was just beginning to forget about her awful hair when Bucky held a bag of cheese curls out to her.

"Have one," said Bucky.

"No, thank you," said Chloe.

"Why not?" said Bucky. "They look just like your hair!"

"They do not!" said Mei-Hua hotly when everybody laughed. "Her hair isn't even orange!"

It was nice that Mei-Hua was such a good friend, but it didn't make Chloe feel any better. She still wished she could hide under the cafeteria table and stay there for the rest of the day.

Chloe washed her hair as soon as she got home. Then she sat down at the kitchen table and wrote her immigrant assignment.

Mei-Hua was the first person Mrs. Mellor picked to read her story. She stood up and read: "Po-Po, my grandmother, told me a story about her mother, who came to America when she was young. My Tai-Po, my great-grandmother, was only twelve when she had to ride on the subway all by herself to pick up some important papers for her father. She was scared to death because she couldn't read or speak a word of English, and she was afraid she would get lost. So my Tai-Po found out how many stops the subway ride was, and she put twelve stones in her right pocket. Every time the train stopped and she saw a sign, she removed a stone and put it in her left pocket. When the pocket was full, she got off."

Mei-Hua paused and looked at the class. "My Tai-Po was very brave. It's scary when you can't talk to anybody or ask for directions. It's like there are two worlds, and you are in one, and everybody else is in another." She sat down quickly and said, "Phew!" to Chloe.

Ilana was next. She stood up and read, "Great-Grandma Rose was in steerage when she came over from Romania on the boat. That's the bottom of the boat, and she told me it was smelly and crowded and lots of people cried and got seasick, including Grandma Rose's mother. An old man told her the word 'lemon,' and Grandma Rose went up to first class where the rich people stayed, and she danced and sang for lemons. Grandma even showed me how she caught the lemons people threw by holding out her apron. Then she gave the lemons to her mother, who sucked on them, and it made her mother feel better. She got teary when she told me, and said I took after her because I'm a good singer."

Mrs. Mellor spoke up. "That was lovely, both of you. These stories have something in common, don't they?"

Mei-Hua raised her hand. "Both grandmas had to do something alone," she said.

Germaine stuck his hand in the air and waved

wildly. "I know, I know. They both helped their parents."

"That's right," said Mrs. Mellor. "And they were both very brave."

Bucky yelled, "Mei-Hua's grandma was braver," but Mrs. Mellor ignored him and called on Chloe.

Chloe stood up. Her hands shook a little as she held the paper. She started reading, and her voice was so low that Mrs. Mellor asked her to speak up.

She read, "My mother was born here, so she wasn't an immigrant. But her mother was, and that's my Grandma Rebecca. Grandma kept some of her old customs, and she packed my mother's lunch box with blintzes and potato pancakes instead of peanut butter and jelly, in weird pieces of paper. Some of the kids made fun of her. The worst time was when she had to wear a babushka to school. That's a Russian kerchief. The kids were mean to her because she wasn't like them. I guess they thought she wasn't cool."

Chloe cleared her throat and said, "I know

what she felt like. I wanted curly hair in the worst way, so my sister Dorothy tried to set it. It was a total mess. Bucky said it looked like a science project, and he was right." The class laughed, and Chloe looked up from her paper at their smiling faces. She continued: "Maybe I would have been better off if I wore a babushka. It's hard when people make fun of you because you look different. Maybe that's why so many immigrants lived together in the same place, so that nobody would laugh at them for being strange. Maybe I should keep my hair straight." Chloe sat down quickly, and stood up again. "Or maybe my sister Dorothy should learn to set hair," she said, and the class started to laugh and clap at the same time.

Mei-Hua leaned over with her short dark hair and gave her the okay sign. Theresa shook her blond curls and said to Bucky, "Chloe's funny!" Bucky said, "I hope I'm not next. I interviewed my dog. He's an Irish setter, so he's an immigrant from Ireland."

Chloe laughed and flicked back her long

21

straight hair. It had looked smooth and shiny in the mirror that morning. Perhaps she wasn't as cute as Harry, but she was funny in her own way. Maybe an eagle's nose and straight hair weren't so bad. She would wear it in a ponytail tomorrow, elf ears and all.

2

Chloe's Card

CHLOE WAS A COLLECTOR. She didn't collect the usual things, like stamps or butterflies or stickers. When she was little and she had dry cereal for breakfast, she always studied the cereal box. And when the box was finished, she wouldn't let her mother throw it away until she had cut out the pretty bowl with the cereal and fruit in it. She had collected fifteen bowl pictures: her Cheerios, her father's wheat flakes (the most boring-looking box), Harry's Lucky Charms, Dorothy's corn puffs (until her mother had decided they had too much sugar in them), Grandma's Shredded

Wheat (which looked so much better than it tasted), Grandpa's bran flakes (which were as boring as Dad's wheat flakes), and several others that the family had tried along the way. Chloe was the only person she knew who had a scrapbook of cereal bowls.

She also collected greeting cards. She had an album crammed full of Mother's Day cards, Father's Day cards, Christmas cards, the best of the Valentine cards because there were so many, Hanukkah cards, get-well cards after Grandma's operation, wedding cards from Aunt Sarah and Uncle Peter, happy anniversary cards from her mother and father, and birthday cards from everybody. Everybody except her little brother Harry, who taped his birthday cards on his wall and left them there until Mrs. Kane could sneak them down. She didn't like the marks they left on the paint.

Grandma Rebecca's birthday was coming up, and Chloe's mother was making a party.

"With crepe paper and balloons?" said Chloe, putting one of the few Thanksgiving cards she had received in her scrapbook next to two other cards with turkeys on them. "I could use a pilgrim," said Chloe. "I'm tired of turkeys."

"How about turkey for Grandma's party? Turkey and my homemade cranberry sauce?" said Mrs. Kane.

"We just had that for Thanksgiving!" said Chloe. "I like your chicken better."

"Thanksgiving is my favorite holiday," said her mother. "I hate when it's over."

"How about pizza?" said Harry, playing with his model cars under the kitchen table.

"Grandma can't eat pizza and neither can Grandpa."

"Oh," said Harry. "They burp."

"Too much cholesterol," said Mrs. Kane, laughing.

"I'll make Grandma a card," said Harry. "With glitter."

"Me, too," said Chloe. "Why don't we make her one big card?"

Harry ran to get Dorothy. Chloe got a large sheet of construction paper folded in half, scissors, glue, colored tissue paper, and three bottles of glitter. They cleared off the kitchen table and started to work.

Chloe gave the orders. "Here, Harry. You tear pieces of the red tissue paper apart, and we'll paste them around the edges. I'll make the design with glue." Chloe swirled a large picture of a heart with a flower in the middle out of glue. "Dorothy, you take the glitter and pour it on."

Dorothy sprinkled the glitter carefully.

Then Chloe slowly lifted the card and walked over to the kitchen sink, trying not to spill the glitter.

"Get glitter in my lettuce, and you'll eat it for supper," said Mrs. Kane, lifting the colander out of the sink.

Chloe shook the piece of paper over the drain, and bits of leftover glitter floated into the basin.

"It looks like sparkling rain," said Harry.

"Harry, you're a poet," said Mrs. Kane.

"I'm the writer," said Chloe. "I'll write the message that goes inside." Chloe put the card back on the table. "You two paste the tissue paper around the edges and then let it dry."

"Supper's in half an hour. I'll expect the table to be cleared by then," said Mrs. Kane.

"Okay," said Chloe, and she took her greeting-card album and went into her bedroom.

Writing a birthday poem was harder than she thought. Chloe sat for a long time. She chewed the end of her pencil. She shredded a piece of paper. She doodled pictures of flowers on another piece. Finally, she wrote down:

Roses are red.

But she couldn't think of anything good to rhyme with *red*. *Fed* was no good. *Bed* was worse. *Dead* was awful. It sounded like a funeral. She wrote down another line.

Violets are blue.

But everybody wrote that. She couldn't think of anything else, so she wrote:

Sugar is sweet.

Chloe thought maybe she could be original with the last line.

And I won't cry boo hoo.
Because it's your birthday.

Awful. Just awful, thought Chloe. The oldest child was supposed to be the smartest, and the smartest grandchild couldn't even write Grandma a birthday poem. She tried once more.

> *Roses are red,*
> *Violets are blue,*
> *Sugar is sweet,*
> *And this card is made with glue.*

Chloe threw the pencil down in disgust. Her grandmother would think she was a two-year-old. Her grandmother wouldn't want to show it to the ladies at temple.

Chloe had an idea. She opened up her greeting-card scrapbook and read some of the cards. They were much better than anything Chloe had written.

She took out a Father's Day card. It said:

> *I've searched the world around me,*
> *From sea to mountaintop,*
> *Through plains and steppes and jungle brush*
> *And now my search must stop.*
> *I send my father's Day greeting,*
> *From north, south, east, and west,*

28

No matter what the vantage point,
Dear father, you're the best.

It was almost what Chloe had wanted to write. Almost what she wanted to tell her grandma on her birthday.

She pulled out a birthday card she had bought for her mother a year ago. It said:

> *For a mother as sweet as you are,*
> *The best in every way,*
> *Whose smile, as bright as sunshine,*
> *Makes life a holiday.*
>
> *For a mother as loved and cherished,*
> *So warm and kind and dear,*
> *May our birthday wishes bless you,*
> *For we love you more each year.*

Now *that* was what Chloe wanted to say to her grandma. How she loved her more each year. Chloe picked up her pencil and crossed out the word *mother* wherever she found it. Then she put in the word *grandma*. She read the poem out loud. It sounded great.

Chloe took out a sheet of pink construction

29

paper and picked out the prettiest violet felt-tip pen. Then she copied the poem with the word *grandma* instead of *mother* onto the paper, in her best handwriting.

"I'm finished!" she announced as she entered the kitchen.

"Read it, read it," said Harry.

"Let's hear it," said Mrs. Kane, wiping her hands on her apron.

"It's a surprise," said Chloe. "You'll all get to hear it when Grandma reads it tomorrow." Then she picked up the homemade greeting card with the glittery heart on it and took it into her room to paste the poem inside.

On Saturday morning, Mrs. Kane took her favorite cookbook down from the shelf and handed it to Chloe.

"Would you like to help me make Grandma's cake?" she said.

"Sure," said Chloe, feeling very special.

"It's a cake that uses a lot of egg whites," said her mother, taking a dozen eggs from the refrigerator. "You can learn how to separate the egg white from the yolk."

"The yolk is the yellow part," said Chloe, feeling smart and grown-up. Dorothy and Harry were much too young to separate eggs.

"Look up angel food cake in the index," said Mrs. Kane. "It's a low cholesterol cake." Chloe's mother lined up the ingredients on the table: sugar, flour, salt, cream of tartar, vanilla, and almond extract. She took out some bowls and showed Chloe how to crack the egg in half and shift the yolk from one half-shell to the other, letting the egg white run over the sides into the bowl. Only once did Chloe break a yolk, and her mother just took a spoon and removed the offending yellow from the bowl of egg whites.

"Wow," said Dorothy, watching Chloe. "You do that great."

Then Mrs. Kane handed Chloe a rotary beater. "Get to work," she said with a smile. "It's better by hand than with the electric mixer."

Chloe turned the handle steadily. She turned and turned until she thought her arm would break off.

"Do you want to try it, Dorothy?" she said. Dorothy beat the egg whites some more, but her hand wasn't as steady as Chloe's. She handed the beater back to Chloe, and Chloe whipped the egg whites until finally the liquid began to stiffen and peak.

Slowly, a tablespoon at a time, her mother added a cup of sugar, then the vanilla and almond extract. They added the sifted flour and sugar and a pinch of salt, and Chloe held the tube pan while her mother poured in the batter. Then Chloe put the pan carefully into the hot oven, without even burning her hands.

"Good work," said her mother. "The cake will be delicious." She kissed Chloe on top of her head. "Thank you, honey," she said.

Everyone was starving by the time Grandma and Grandpa arrived. Mr. Kane had put the extra leaf in the table, and Harry was the first person to sit down.

"Chicken, chicken, chicken," chanted Harry as he banged the handle of his fork on the table.

"No banging on the table," said Mr. Kane as he set down a steaming plate of honey-glazed chicken.

"I was drumming," said Harry, laughing. "So can I have the drumstick?"

"No drumming," said Harry's father. He put a chicken leg on Harry's plate and called out to Chloe. "Chloe, do you want the other leg?"

"Yes, please," said Chloe, walking Grandma to the table. "I made the cake," she whispered to Grandma. "And I wrote the card."

"How wonderful," said Grandma, kissing Chloe on the cheek. "I got lipstick on you." Grandma rubbed her thumb on Chloe's smudged cheek. "You're getting so grown-up," said Grandma.

After dinner, everybody helped clear the table.

"Mother, you sit down," said Mrs. Kane to Grandma. "You're the birthday girl."

"The faster I clear," said Grandma, "the faster I get to eat Chloe's cake!"

"Rebecca, sit down," said Grandpa. "They have to light the candles."

Harry stood guard over the light switch, and Dorothy put the candles in their holders. Chloe arranged the candles on the cake, and her mother lit them.

"Okay, Harry," said Mrs. Kane, and Harry switched off the lights. The angel food cake glowed in the darkness and Mrs. Kane set it in front of Grandma.

They all sang "Happy Birthday," and Grandma blew out the candles. "My wish has already come true," said Grandma as she took the first piece of cake. "As light as a feather," she said, putting a forkful into her mouth. "And my granddaughter made it!"

At last it was time for the presents. Grandma's face was pink as she opened up a large package wrapped in shiny silver paper.

"Faster, Grandma," said Harry, but Grandma took her time, peeling the tape off slowly so that it didn't make a mark.

"I can iron it and save it," said Grandma as she handed the paper to Grandpa Leon.

Mrs. Kane laughed and shook her head. "I hope it fits," she said.

Grandma pulled out a long apricot-colored nightgown with pale yellow ribbons at the top. She let out a stream of *ooohs* and *ahhhs* and said, "It's much too beautiful to wear!"

"You'd better wear it," said Mrs. Kane, and

she motioned to Chloe to bring out the next present.

Chloe handed Grandma the glittery card. "Read it, Grandma," she said.

Grandma read the card out loud.

> "For a grandma as sweet as you are,
> The best in every way,
> Whose smile, as bright as sunshine,
> Makes life a holiday.

> "For a grandma as loved and cherished,
> So warm and kind and dear,
> May our birthday wishes bless you,
> For we love you more each year."

Grandma closed the card. "You wrote that, Chloe?" she said. "It's the most beautiful card I ever got." Grandma stood up from her chair, walked over to Chloe, and kissed her. Chloe could feel tears on her cheek.

"I put the tissue paper on," said Harry. And Grandma walked over and kissed Harry.

"The red tissue paper is wonderful," said Grandma.

"I poured the glitter on the glue," said Dorothy.

"It's the most terrific glitter design I've ever seen," said Grandma, kissing Dorothy. "Thank you, everyone, for the nicest birthday I can remember."

It was late when Grandma and Grandpa went home. The dishwasher was whirring away. Harry's face was the color of honey-glazed chicken, and Mrs. Kane helped him take a bath. Mr. Kane put away the remains of the angel food cake and sat down to read the newspaper. Dorothy watched television.

Chloe went to her room and didn't do anything. She had a nagging feeling in her head. She remembered Grandma's tears when Grandma kissed her. She loved the compliments and the praise everyone gave her. But now she wished she'd just written, "I love you, Grandma," inside the glittery card.

She could hear the sounds of Dorothy and Harry going to bed. "One more drink of water," called Harry.

"One more book," called Dorothy.

"I have to go to the bathroom," called Harry.

"You went already," Mr. Kane called back.

"I have to go again," Harry answered.

Chloe could hear her father sigh as he got up to turn on the bathroom light. She could hear her mother leave Dorothy's room and say, "No more books. It's bedtime."

She was grown-up and didn't need her parents to visit her room anymore. After all, she made an angel food cake, practically all by herself. She wrote a fancy poem. Or did she? Chloe felt like a liar.

There was a knock on her bedroom door.

"Chloe?" said her mother, opening the door a crack.

Chloe didn't answer.

"You're very quiet in there," said her mother. "Can I come in?"

"I guess," said Chloe, wishing she could say no.

Her mother entered the room. "Why is it so dark in here?" she said. "Is something the matter?" Mrs. Kane perched on the edge of the bed.

Chloe shrugged her shoulders.

"Grandma loved the poem you wrote. She couldn't stop talking about it."

"It wasn't so great," said Chloe.

"I thought it was wonderful."

"You only love me if I do wonderful things," said Chloe.

Chloe's mother looked hurt. "That's not true," she said. "I love you because . . . well, you're not Harry and you're not Dorothy—you're you."

"I'm a liar," said Chloe. "I didn't write that card."

"Oh," said her mother. She was silent for a minute. "It was brave of you to tell me."

"I feel just awful," said Chloe.

"I know," said her mother. "Why don't you talk to Grandma?"

"I couldn't," said Chloe. "She'll never like me again."

"I don't think anything could make her feel that way, honey." Mrs. Kane cupped her hand under Chloe's chin. "Try calling Grandma," she said.

Chloe's heart hammered away as she dialed Grandma's number.

"Hello?" said Grandma.

"Hello," said Chloe, certain that Grandma could hear her heart beating.

"What is it, darling?" said Grandma.

"It's the card I gave you," said Chloe, taking a deep breath. "I didn't write the poem, and I'm sorry I made you think I did."

"I see," said Grandma. She paused. "Do you remember what I said when I blew out my candles?"

"No," said Chloe, more miserable than when Bucky said her hair reminded him of cheese curls.

"I said that my wish had already come true. Before I even read your card."

"What was your wish?" said Chloe.

"That I spend my birthday with my grandchildren and children, with the people I love."

"But the poem, Grandma," said Chloe.

Grandma said something in Yiddish that must have been a swear word, because Grandpa shushed her in the background.

"Excuse me," said Grandma. "But who cares about the card? Did you mean what you wrote?"

"Every word, Grandma," said Chloe.

"I thought so," said Grandma. "I tasted it in the cake. Now go to sleep, Chloe. You'll write me another poem next year."

"I love you, Grandma," said Chloe.

"I love you, too," said Grandma.

Chloe hung up the phone. She opened the refrigerator door and looked inside. She took out the carton of milk and poured herself a glassful. Then she unwrapped the last piece of angel food cake and ate it. It was as light as a feather.

3

Mrs. Kane's Tummy Ache

THE DAY AFTER Grandma's party, Mrs. Kane drank tea at breakfast instead of coffee.

"Are you sick, Mama?" said Chloe, because Mrs. Kane gave everybody tea with honey if they weren't feeling well, even though Harry said he'd only drink it with a scoop of vanilla fudge ice cream in it.

"I'm not feeling myself," said Mrs. Kane. "Does anyone else have a stomachache?"

Chloe and Harry were eating their third pancakes, and Dorothy was on her fourth because she'd had a head start, so it was a bit of a silly question.

After breakfast, Mrs. Kane stayed in the bathroom for a long time. Harry the detective ran into the living room where the girls were watching cartoons.

"I think she's throwing up," whispered Harry. "It's the same noise I made the day we went to the beach when I threw up in the car and we had to park in the field and wash it all out."

"Don't remind me," said Chloe, rubbing her stomach. "I've just had four pancakes!"

"But don't you remember, Chloe? We got back into the car and you said you were feeling sick, and Dorothy said the smell was going to make her throw up, too, and Mama said she didn't want a chain reaction, and I said, 'What's a chain reaction?'"

The girls started to scream, but that didn't stop Harry. "And Mama had the idea of putting baby powder all over the bottom of the car and everybody started sneezing because it was blowing in our faces with the car windows open. Don't you remember?"

"We remember, we remember!" shouted Chloe

and Dorothy, waving him out of the room.

"Well, Mama is making the same noises." Harry the detective turned and trotted back into the hallway where he bumped into Mr. Kane.

"Mama is . . ."

"I know, Harry," said his father. "I'm going to take her to see the doctor as soon as she gets out of the bathroom."

"Great!" said Harry. "I can bring my doctor's kit."

"Not today, Harry. Grandpa Leon is going to stay with you until we get back."

As soon as the doorbell rang, Harry swung the door open and said to a surprised Grandpa, "You're sick, Grandpa. Lie down on the couch and I'll be your doctor."

Grandpa did as he was told. He walked into the living room, said hello to Chloe and Dorothy, took off his shoes, and lay down on the couch. He started moaning right away. "Oy, Doctor, Doctor, I'm sick, I'm sick."

Mrs. Kane stood in the doorway with her coat on. "Oh, my heavens," she said, looking at

Grandpa. "It must have been the chicken. I've poisoned everybody with my chicken."

Chloe turned around and said, "It could have been my angel food cake, Mama."

Harry arrived with his doctor's kit and said, "We're pretending, Mama. Are there any M&Ms left from Halloween? I need them as medicine for Grandpa."

Mrs. Kane looked relieved, but she brought Harry breath mints. "These will have to do," she said.

"I hate mints," said Harry.

"I thought they were for the patient!" said Mrs. Kane, laughing.

Mr. Kane took her arm and said, "The sooner we get to the doctor's, the sooner we'll get home," and they waved good-bye.

"Feel better," called Chloe. She thought throwing up was the very worst thing in the world, much worse than a cold or a sore throat, because you didn't feel like eating.

Chloe and Dorothy were enlisted by Harry to be nurses. Dorothy said, "You can call me Nurse

Nightingale." She had just learned about Florence Nightingale in school.

Chloe said, "Call me Doctor Kane," because she refused to be bossed around by her younger sister.

Harry bandaged up Grandpa's leg, and Dorothy held a stethoscope to his heart. "You're a little fast," she told Grandpa, and when he started to laugh, Harry told him that too much excitement was not good for him.

Unfortunately, Grandpa would not take Harry's pills. "I don't like mints, either," he whispered to Chloe, so Chloe ran into the kitchen and brought back some Goldfish snacks which Grandpa started munching by the handful. "Some seltzer, Doctor," he said to Harry. Harry dragged the bottle in and Dorothy poured some into the toy pill bottle and said, "Drink this. It will make you feel better."

"Pardon me?" said Grandpa. "I think my hearing is going."

"I'm the ear specialist," said Chloe, and she took a flashlight and peered into Grandpa's ears.

45

"You've got wax," she told him.

"Do you know what else he has?" said Harry, pointing to Grandpa's ears.

"What?" said Chloe.

"He has elf ears, just like yours!"

"He does!" said Dorothy excitedly.

"You have wax," said Chloe, ignoring them both.

Grandpa started laughing so hard that his face turned very pink. "I paid my doctor yesterday for the same diagnosis!" he sputtered. "He never told me I had elf ears, but he said I had wax!"

Chloe looked very pleased. "Well," she said, holding out her hand, "you'll have to pay me, too."

Grandpa fished in his pocket for some change, and he made Chloe take fifty cents for her diagnosis, even though she said she was only kidding. Then he gave Harry and Dorothy the same amount. "For my leg doctor, and my heart doctor," he said. "Cheap at the price."

Harry told Grandpa that watching "Teenage Mutant Ninja Turtles" would make him feel as good as new.

"I won't watch," said Chloe, folding her arms.

"Why not?" said Grandpa, looking surprised. "Too violent?"

"No," said Chloe. "I wrote a letter to the station because the only girls in the program are the girls the turtles rescue."

"What about April?" said Harry.

"She doesn't count. Anyway, girls can save themselves. They don't always need some dumb turtle to help them."

"I agree," said Dorothy, folding her arms just the way Chloe had.

"Well," said Grandpa. "What was their reply?"

"They said they're trying, but boys won't watch girl cartoons. Can you believe it? They expect us to watch James Bond, Jr., and Garfield the Cat, who is obviously a boy, and Dennis the Menace and G.I. Joe, and boys won't watch girl cartoons." Chloe's face was as pink as Grandpa's had been.

"You forgot 'Ghostbusters' and 'Bobby's World,'" said Harry.

"And Tom and Jerry," said Dorothy. "Even if

one of them is a cat and one of them is a mouse."

"I'm appalled!" said Grandpa. He turned to Harry. "I'm afraid I have to boycott this program," he said.

"What does boycott mean?" asked Harry.

"Refuse to watch it," said Grandpa.

"Hmmph!" said Harry, looking miffed. Then his eyes lit up. "You can't boycott it, Grandpa!"

"Why not?"

"Because you'll have to girlcott it! Get it?"

They boycotted it anyway, and watched a nature film, which everyone enjoyed even if Harry was pretending he was a dolphin and making dolphin noises. Grandpa said he'd make some tuna-fish sandwiches for lunch, and Harry said, "Only the kind that says they don't kill dolphins."

Grandpa rummaged in the closet and showed Harry a can that said OUR NETS ARE DOLPHIN-FREE.

"Thank goodness," said Chloe. "Now he won't boycott the tuna fish!"

"Girlcott it, girlcott it!" said Harry, and everybody laughed.

They were eating tuna-fish sandwiches when Mr. and Mrs. Kane walked in. Mrs. Kane sniffed and said, "What's that fishy smell?" Then she ran into the bathroom again.

"What's the matter with her?" said Chloe.

"I'll let your mother tell you," said Mr. Kane.

Mrs. Kane emerged, white-faced with just a touch of green. "Could someone move that bowl of tuna fish away?" she said in a small voice.

"It's dolphin-free," said Harry.

"I'm sure," said Mrs. Kane. "Your father and I have something to tell you."

"It's a bit of a shock," added Mr. Kane.

Chloe started getting worried. Ilana Levy's mother had once had an operation in the hospital, and her grouchy aunt came to stay with her for a week, and Ilana had a terrible time.

Mrs. Kane must have noticed Chloe's worried look, because she said quickly, "It's good news, I think."

"You think?" said Harry.

Mrs. Kane took a big breath. "I'm going to have a baby."

Except for the hum of the refrigerator, there was dead silence in the kitchen.

Grandpa spoke up first. "Well! What do you think of that!"

"I'll have to call Mother," said Mrs. Kane.

"Forget about it," said Harry.

"Grandma will want to know," said his father.

"Forget about it," Harry repeated. He looked like he was going to cry.

"I think he means the baby," said Chloe.

"It'll be fun, Harry," said Mrs. Kane. "A new baby is like a new . . . present!"

"I don't want a new present!" shouted Harry, and he ran out of the room.

Mrs. Kane stared at Mr. Kane. "I'll go," he said, but Chloe and Dorothy had already jumped up from the table.

"I think we can understand better," explained Chloe.

Harry was curled up in a ball on his bed, clutching the plastic palm tree that used to belong to his pet turtle Personality before he died.

"It's okay, Harry," said Chloe softly.

"We'll be here," said Dorothy.

50

Harry mumbled something, and Chloe lay down next to him and put her head right next to his. "What did you say, Harry?"

He whispered something and then said quite clearly, "I want to be alone."

"What did he say?" said Dorothy.

"He said he won't be the baby anymore."

Dorothy addressed the curled-up lump on the bed. "You'll still be our baby," she said. "When we play house, you can still be the baby."

Harry sat bolt upright and said loudly, "I don't want to be the baby in your dumb old house games."

"Suit yourself," said Chloe, trying not to get angry. "How about we ask Mom if we can have some vanilla fudge ice cream for dessert?"

Harry considered the idea and said, "All right."

But as Chloe and Dorothy turned to leave the room, Harry called after them, "I'm boycotting the baby anyway!"

Chloe knew what Harry meant, but she was too old to boycott a baby.

She and Dorothy returned to the kitchen and told Mr. and Mrs. Kane about Harry's boycott.

"I just realized," said Dorothy. "I won't be the middle child anymore!"

Chloe munched on a cookie. "I'll always be the oldest, no matter how many babies we have."

"Maybe it will be twins!" said Dorothy.

"Or triplets!" said Chloe.

"Please," said Mrs. Kane, nibbling on a saltine. "Just let me eat my cracker in peace."

"Sucking on a lemon is good for seasickness," Chloe told her mother.

"Thank you, Chloe," said Mrs. Kane, although she looked like she had no intention of sucking on a lemon.

Harry appeared and sat down at the kitchen table. "I'm ready for my vanilla fudge ice cream," he said.

Mrs. Kane let out a moan.

"Are you sick again?" said Mr. Kane anxiously.

"No," said Mrs. Kane with a sigh. "We're out of vanilla fudge ice cream."

Harry looked the way he did when his best friend Benjamin broke his favorite water pistol. He rested his head on the table.

"How about some peach frozen yogurt?" said Mrs. Kane.

Harry lifted his head. He glared at his mother, his father, and his two sisters. Then he walked out of the room, calling over his shoulder, "I'm boycotting the baby!" There were thumping footsteps on the stairs as he shouted, "And I'm boycotting frozen yogurt, too!"

Grandpa looked at Mrs. Kane. "I'm sorry I taught him that word," he said.

4

Chloe in the Know

WHEN CHLOE TOLD her best friend Mei-Hua about Mrs. Kane's tummy ache, Mei-Hua rolled her eyes.

It was a terrible shock to Chloe, because everybody else was so excited when they heard the news. Aunt Sarah laughed and cried at the same time. Grandma Rebecca started to dance, until Grandpa Leon said, "Use your cane, Miss Twinkletoes."

Grandma said, "My arthritis has disappeared from the joy of it."

"Good," said Mr. Kane. "You can come and

do the feeding in the middle of the night." Chloe wasn't sure if he was joking or not.

But Mei-Hua rolled her eyes and said, "You're in for it."

"In for what?" Chloe was only three when Harry was born, so she didn't really remember what it was like.

"You'll be helping your mother so much, you won't have time to play."

Chloe's heart sank. She was just getting used to the idea of having a cute little baby around the house. A cuddly sweet baby, not one like Harry, who just yesterday had pulled the head off her favorite Barbie doll because he was mad at her.

"I thought you liked having a baby sister," said Chloe. "You told me it was better than having a Baby Cries Real Tears doll. I thought we could wheel them around together."

"Are you kidding?" said Mei-Hua. "My mother wouldn't let me take Mei-Lun out by myself."

"Oh." Chloe watched Mrs. Mellor walk in.

She wrote two words on the blackboard: "personal narrative." "We're in for it, all right," said Chloe, but Mei-Hua wasn't looking.

Mei-Hua was saying, "My mother lets me help her change all those smelly diapers, that's for sure. She lets me clean up all of the baby's messes. And she lets the baby wreck my room!"

"Oh," repeated Chloe. She was glad when Mrs. Mellor tapped on the blackboard.

"We're going to continue working on our writing," said Mrs. Mellor. "For tomorrow, I'd like a story about a personal experience, with feelings and with voice. Please don't go home and write about a green monster or a fairy princess. Write something about yourselves, something that your family did together, something you enjoy or don't enjoy. Remember, I want a personal narrative. I want your own feelings."

Chloe sighed. Mrs. Mellor was big on feelings. How about, "I feel like the bottom of my brother Harry's turtle bowl when he forgot to clean it out." Would that do? Or "I feel like throwing all my school books in the garbage can." Would that make Mrs. Mellor happy? Or "I feel like running away from babies and saltine crackers and grouchy brothers and Mellor the Yeller." What if your feelings were all rotten?

After school, Chloe settled herself at the kitchen table. Harry was watching cartoons, and Dorothy was in her room with the door closed and her NO ENTRY sign hanging on the doorknob. Chloe chewed on her pencil. It was hard getting started when the only feelings you had were mad feelings. She thought maybe some milk and cookies would help.

Chloe peered into the refrigerator and found the milk. The carton was empty. "Where's all the milk?" she called to Harry.

"Gone!" said Harry, eyes glued to the television set.

Chloe looked in the cabinet. She found raisins, flour, spaghetti sauce, juice boxes. Everything but cookies. "Where are the cookies?" she shouted.

"Dorothy and I were starved!" Harry shouted back.

Chloe stormed off to the bathroom. Harry

scooted ahead of her and shut the door.

"Beat you!" said Harry.

"I've had it!" said Chloe, knocking on Dorothy's door and walking in without waiting for an answer.

Dorothy slid something off her desk and onto her lap. "What do you want?" she said quickly.

"What are you hiding?" said Chloe.

"Nothing." Dorothy draped her skirt over a flat box.

"My glitter pens!" said Chloe. "I was looking for them!" She grabbed the box from Dorothy and walked out of the room. "I have a sneak for a sister and a rat for a brother!" she said in a loud voice.

"I was only borrowing them!" answered Dorothy.

"I was about to have an accident," said Harry.

"Sure," Chloe said under her breath as she sat down at the table again. Mrs. Mellor never said not to write about angry feelings. Chloe picked up her pencil.

She finished just as Mrs. Kane walked in.

"What are you working on?" said her mother. "May I read it?"

Don't show her, Chloe said to herself, but she handed the paper to her mother anyway.

As Mrs. Kane read, her face got paler and paler. Chloe's face got redder and redder. She fixed her eyes on her mother's wrinkled-up brow. Maybe it wasn't such a good idea writing about angry feelings—especially when you had to watch your mother's feelings get hurt.

Mrs. Kane read:

My name is Chloe Kane, and I'm the oldest. I was born first, I burped first, I talked first, I fell off the bed first. I did everything first. I was the first one to go to kindergarten, which sounds easy enough, but it was scary because every day at lunchtime the monitor ate my cookies. Finally the teacher caught him and he stopped. When Billy Zimmer peed in Harry's locker every day for a week, Harry told me and I told the teacher, and it stopped. He didn't have to wait a month, like I did. At Dr. Weiss's, my mother lines us all up for our shots. Guess who has to go first? Me. I have to unpack groceries because Harry runs away. I have to wait for the bathroom because someone is always sneaking ahead. I have to go to sleep at the same time as Harry and Dorothy because they stay up singing in bed. I have to watch stupid videos because they never let me pick. And when the new baby comes, I'll have to change diapers and clean up messes and baby-sit. That's what I'm told, and I believe it. It's just not fair. If I could go on strike, I would. But I can't, because I'm the oldest.

Mrs. Kane handed Chloe the piece of paper. Her eyes had a pained look in them. "I didn't know you felt this way, sweetheart," she said.

Chloe hung her head.

"It will be all right," said Mrs. Kane. "I promise you. The baby isn't going to ruin your life. Okay?"

"Okay," said Chloe, but she didn't look in her mother's eyes. How could her mother be so certain that her life wouldn't be ruined?

"It was very well written, honey," said her mother. "And I'm so glad I found out how you feel. But I would never let you baby-sit. You're much too young."

While her mother started dinner, Chloe wrote,

By the way, my mother says I'm too young to baby-sit. So what happens in three or four years?

After that, Chloe noticed that Mrs. Kane didn't ask her to do much of anything. She told Dorothy to get her a roll of paper towels from the closet, and after Harry skedaddled when she was unpacking the groceries, she ran after him and said he could at least put away the cereal. She even let Chloe stay up to watch *Bye Bye Birdie* on television so that Dorothy and Harry were actually sleeping when she went to bed.

When Mrs. Mellor returned the class's papers, she had written *Very Good* in red pencil at the top of the page. At the bottom she added,

Chloe—I have three sisters and a brother of my own, and I wouldn't give them up for the world. It seems hard now, but you'll

61

realize how lucky you are when you get older.

"How did you do?" whispered Mei-Hua.

"She liked it," said Chloe. "How did you do?"

"Excellent!" said Mei-Hua, handing her the paper.

Chloe read:

My sister Mei-Lun is only thirteen months old, but I think she's the smartest baby in the world. When she stacks blocks, she looks at me and says, 'Ma-Ha! Ma-Ha!' until she gets my attention. It's so cute the way she can't pronounce my name. Then she claps and I clap until she knocks them down and we do it all over again. My mother says that Mei-Lun idolizes me because I'm her big sister. I think that Mei-Lun makes my life special, because she makes me feel special.

Chloe was amazed. "What about changing the smelly diapers and not ever getting to play?" she said.

"Oh, that," said Mei-Hua, waving her hand.

Chloe thought it was all very confusing.

Chloe's mother was talking on the telephone about baby names. Chloe couldn't remember when her mother didn't talk about the baby, whose name had been narrowed down to Chelsea or Lauren or Sky if it was a girl, and Michael or Sam or Dakota if it was a boy. Mrs. Kane kept crossing the names Dakota and Sky off the list, but Mr. Kane kept putting them back on. "I'm not giving birth to a cowboy," she told him. Harry said that he was the only cowboy in the family. He suggested that the baby be called Fat Belly.

"I'm over thirty-five, Mother." Mrs. Kane spoke into the telephone. "The doctor says I should have the test." Mrs. Kane nodded her head, as if Grandma Rebecca was sitting there drinking coffee with her. "No," said Chloe's mother. "I'm not sure if I want to find out or not. Maybe it should be a surprise."

"Maybe what should be a surprise?" said Chloe as her mother hung up the phone.

"Whether the baby is a girl or a boy. On Saturday I'm going for a test called amniocentesis, to see if the baby is healthy, and they can let me know the sex of the baby."

"And you don't want to know?" Chloe was amazed. If anyone handed her a present that said NOT TO BE OPENED UNTIL YOUR BIRTHDAY, she would have to open it the minute she got home.

"I'm not sure," said Mrs. Kane. "It was so exciting when you and Dorothy and Harry were born, not knowing what you would be!"

"But we could find out if Harry or Dorothy has to share a room or not!" There was no way Chloe was going to sleep next to a baby and a bunch of dirty diapers.

Mrs. Kane shrugged. "As long as it's healthy. We'll see. Your father will be with me, and we can decide when I'm there."

But on the morning of Mrs. Kane's appointment, just as she'd finished drinking what looked to Chloe like a gallon of water, Mr. Kane rolled out of bed and said, "I think I'm going to faint."

Mrs. Kane took his temperature and said, "Get

64

back into bed. You have the flu." Then she called Grandma and Grandpa, but they weren't at home. "I'd like some company," she said out loud, "but I know Aunt Sarah is working."

"I'll go," said Chloe.

"I'll go," said Dorothy, who had just gotten up and was still in her pajamas.

"I'll go," said Harry, who didn't even know where he would be going.

Mrs. Kane thought for a minute. Then she said, "Chloe will go. She's the oldest."

Chloe threw on her coat and got into the car next to her mother. Mrs. Kane squeezed her hand and said, "I'm glad you're coming with me. I'm nervous."

Chloe wasn't used to hearing her mother talk like that. It reminded her of Dorothy when she had had butterflies in her stomach each time she had to speak in front of the class. Except Dorothy was only a little girl at the time. Her mother was . . . well, her mother was a mother!

They sat in the waiting room with several other pregnant ladies. Mrs. Kane rubbed her stomach in a circular motion. She looked at her watch. Then she wriggled in her seat, just like Harry did when he had to go to the bathroom. Only Harry would say, "I can't hold it in any longer!" Chloe remembered the gallon of water she'd seen her mother drink. She hoped her mother wouldn't embarrass her by saying the same thing.

At last a man in a white coat called out, "Kane!"

Chloe and her mother jumped out of their seats and followed him down a long hallway. "Put this on," he said, handing Mrs. Kane a faded pink hospital gown. Chloe waited while her mother got undressed.

"Ready," said Mrs. Kane to the man, who turned out to be the laboratory technician and had a smile like Grandpa Leon's.

Mrs. Kane lay down on a table. The man sat Chloe on a stool next to her mother. "What's your name, honey?" he said.

"Chloe," whispered Chloe.

"That's funny. My name is Joey!" he said.

Mrs. Kane smiled and said, "Chloe's my eldest child. I'm very proud of her."

"So you're going to be a big sister!" said Joey, as if he were handing her an ice cream sundae.

"I'm already a big sister," said Chloe. She wanted to tell him it was no big deal, but Joey was smearing some gooky-looking jelly on her mother's stomach and placing something that looked like a microphone on top.

"Now we can see pictures of the baby on my trusty little machine," said Joey.

Chloe focused her eyes on the screen, which reminded her a little of a television set.

Joey took a conductor's baton out of his lab coat and pointed at a fuzzy black image on the screen. "That's the head!" he said.

Chloe looked hard. She couldn't see much of anything. She squinted.

"There are the arms, and there is the back," said Joey.

Chloe squinted again.

"I can't believe it!" said her mother. "Can you see it, honey?"

67

Chloe stared at the screen, and the image shifted. "There it is," said Chloe excitedly. "But what's it doing?"

"What do you think?" said Joey.

"Is the baby sucking its thumb?"

"Absolutely," said Joey, smiling.

Chloe grinned from ear to ear. Then she took her longest, hardest look at the baby.

"Isn't it amazing?" said Mrs. Kane.

Chloe didn't answer. She stared at the baby, sucking its thumb on the screen. Finally she said, "He looks like Harry."

"Like Harry?" said Mrs. Kane, pushing up on her elbows. "Do you think so?" she said, squinting at the picture. She turned toward Joey. "Is it a boy?" whispered Mrs. Kane.

"Do you really want to know?" said Joey.

Mrs. Kane looked at Chloe. Chloe smiled widely. Her deep-set brown eyes, as beautiful as Mr. Ritter's cocker spaniel's, were bright with excitement.

Mrs. Kane took a deep breath. "We want to know," she said.

"I think Chloe's right," said Joey. "In my opinion, Chloe is going to have a new brother. When the lab results come in, they'll let you know for sure."

Then Joey helped Chloe off the stool and put her behind a white curtain.

"I'll come and get you in a minute," he said. "Sit tight."

Chloe knew they were giving her mother a needle and didn't want her to watch. She could hear her mother say, "Is it over? Did you do it yet?" Chloe held her breath, and listened for the sound of her mother screaming "Ouch!" A new voice said, "All set. We'll just take some more pictures of the baby." Before Chloe knew it, she was back with her mother, who was sitting on the table looking relieved.

When they got home, Chloe and her mother went straight to the bedroom, where Mr. Kane was lying in bed with his eyes closed.

"Hank?" whispered Mrs. Kane.

Mr. Kane opened his eyes. "You're home!" he

said faintly, pulling himself up into a sitting position.

"Let me get some pillows behind you," said Mrs. Kane.

Chloe punched one of her mother's pillows into shape the way she'd seen a nurse do on television, and placed it behind her father's head.

"Is that better?" said Chloe.

"That's great," said Mr. Kane. "How did it go?"

Mrs. Kane perched on the edge of the bed. "It didn't hurt at all," she said.

"I was hidden behind a curtain, and Mama didn't scream or anything," said Chloe.

"Your mother's a trouper," said Mr. Kane proudly, "and so are you!"

"And I saw the baby sucking its thumb!" said Chloe.

"No kidding!" said her father.

"It was amazing," said her mother.

"Can you beat that?" said Mr. Kane. "That's modern technology for you."

"He looked like Harry," said Chloe.

70

Mr. Kane leaned forward. "Like Harry?" he said.

"He did!" said Mrs. Kane. "So I asked the technician, and he said he thinks it's a boy. You're not upset that we found out, are you, Hank?"

"Upset?" said Mr. Kane, smiling so broadly that he hardly looked sick. "Is it really a boy?"

"We won't know for sure until they call us with the test results," said Mrs. Kane, taking her husband's hand.

"But Joey was almost positive," said Chloe.

Mr. Kane squeezed his wife's hand. "A boy," he said, bright-eyed. "We'd better not tell Dorothy or Harry until we're sure. Can you keep a secret, Chloe?"

"I'm very responsible," said Chloe, feeling proud of herself. "I won't tell a soul."

"My son, Dakota," said Mr. Kane dreamily. "It sounds nice, doesn't it?"

Chloe thought she saw her mother roll her eyes. She knew that Harry might like a new brother, but never another cowboy in the family.

71

And Dorothy was big on nicknames, but how could you shorten Dakota?

"Dad?" said Chloe. "I'm the oldest, and I know about these things."

"What?" said Mr. Kane, looking worried.

"You'll have to trust me on this one," she continued.

"Tell me!" said Mr. Kane. "Don't keep me in suspense!"

Chloe took her father's hand. "He doesn't look anything like a Dakota," she said. "He looks like a Michael."

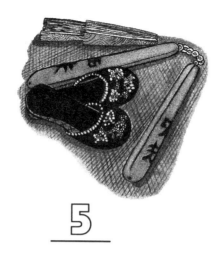

5

Chloe's Class Trip

BY THE TIME she had reached the fourth grade, Chloe had gone with her class to a pumpkin farm, a children's museum, a Native American museum, a museum of natural history, a cooking school, the firehouse, the library, a marionette show, and several plays.

So when Mrs. Mellor announced that they would be taking a very special class trip, Chloe whispered to Mei-Hua, "I wonder what it could be!"

Mei-Hua smiled mysteriously. "I already know," she said.

Mrs. Mellor looked at her watch. "Our visitor should be here any minute," she said, when in walked a tiny lady wearing a red beret and matching red lipstick. She was carrying a bag with pretty Chinese writing on it, filled with oranges.

Mrs. Mellor said something in the lady's ear, and the lady smiled. Her red lipstick made her teeth look very white. "Class," said Mrs. Mellor, "you know that we welcome your parents to visit us and read stories or demonstrate a talent, or tell us about their jobs. Today I'd like you to meet our very special guest, who happens to be Mei-Hua's mother, Mrs. Lee."

Chloe knew Mrs. Lee from play dates at her house, but today she looked different. "Your mom looks pretty!" Chloe whispered to Mei-Hua. Her friend smiled proudly. "But I thought she was a nurse," Chloe said.

"She is," whispered Mei-Hua, just before Mrs. Mellor shushed them.

So what were the oranges for? Maybe she was giving a talk about nutrition. Perhaps they would all practice being surgeons by cutting up an orange. Or maybe Mrs. Lee had a talent for juggling!

"Joe sun!" said Mei-Hua's mother, which was another surprise, because Chloe had spoken to Mrs. Lee lots of times, and she knew how to speak English.

"That means good morning," said Mrs. Lee. "Can you all wish me a good morning?"

"Joe sun!" cried the class. Chloe noticed that Mei-Hua shouted it the loudest of them all.

"Gung hay fat choy!" said Mrs. Lee, only this time everybody repeated, *"Gung hay fat choy!"* without being told.

"Thank you," said Mrs. Lee. "You've just wished me happiness and good fortune."

Chloe couldn't wait to tell Harry, *"Fat choy."* He would probably run to their mother like a crybaby and say that Chloe was calling him names. Then she could say she was wishing Harry good fortune in Chinese!

"The Chinese New Year is our biggest holiday," said Mrs. Lee. "It lasts for fifteen days, and during that time, we're supposed to do good deeds. No swearing or cursing or fighting."

Chloe wondered if Mei-Hua's mother could read minds. Just in case, she decided she wouldn't say *fat choy* to Harry.

Mrs. Lee continued. "Can anyone guess what our lucky color is?" she said, pointing to her hat.

"Red!" the class called out in unison.

"Right!" said Mrs. Lee. "Red is the color of happiness. When I was a little girl, my mother used to dress me all in red, from head to foot—dress, stockings, hat, and shoes. One day, some children taunted me and called me 'Baby Santa Claus!' and for the next few days I wore red and hated it. But now I have children of my own, and I want them to continue in the old Chinese tradition."

Everybody looked at Mei-Hua, who stuck her foot in the air and waved a red shoe! "I don't hate wearing red!" said Mei-Hua.

Her mother smiled. "Mei-Hua especially likes the Chinese New Year because the children receive money in pretty red envelopes."

"And the food's great!" said Mei-Hua.

"That's right," said her mother. "We cook up a feast!"

"Like Christmas dinner!" said Theresa.

"Like when my grandma comes," said Bucky, "because my mother hates to cook."

Mrs. Lee laughed. "We celebrate the Chinese New Year to honor and remember our ancestors. Next week, Mei-Hua and I would like you to share in our tradition and come to Chinatown with us."

The class cheered until Mrs. Mellor held out her hands and motioned for quiet. "Are there any questions for Mrs. Lee?" she said.

Theresa raised her hand. "What does Mei-Hua stand for?" she asked.

"Why don't you tell them, Mei-Hua?"

Mei-Hua stood up and said, "Mei means beautiful America, and Hua means bright and brilliant. It also means to show respect to America but not to forget China, where my ancestors came from. My mother's whole name is Lee Moo-Lan, which I think is even prettier."

"Moo-Lan is my first name, and Lee is my last," said Mrs. Lee. "In Chinese, the last name comes first."

Bucky raised his hand and waved it excitedly. "Does Moo-Lan mean cow?" he said. Chloe couldn't tell if Bucky was joking or not.

Mrs. Lee wasn't offended. "Moo means wood, which stands for strength, and Lan means orchid."

"Which stands for pretty?" said Bucky.

"Yes," said Mrs. Lee, smiling.

"You forgot to tell them that this year is the Year of the Dog," said Mei-Hua.

"Oh, yes. Each year is named for an animal, and every twelve years the cycle begins again. . . . Horse, sheep, monkey, rooster, dog . . ."

Bucky started to bark like a dog, until Mrs. Mellor asked him if he'd like to spend the Chinese New Year in the principal's office.

Mrs. Lee thanked them and was about to leave when she remembered the oranges. She and Mei-Hua gave each child in the class an orange and a pair of chopsticks. "The orange is a symbol of good luck," said Mrs. Lee.

"Maybe if I eat this for lunch, I'll get an A on my math test," whispered Bucky.

"Studying would help," Ilana whispered back.

"You'll probably get a C," whispered Chloe. "For vitamin C!"

Mrs. Lee showed them how to use their chopsticks and had them practice on their erasers. "Next week, when we go to the Chinese restaurant in Chinatown, you'll know how to use these!" She smiled at the class. *"Joy gen!"* she said. "That means good-bye."

"Joy gen!" said the class, and they put their oranges and chopsticks in their knapsacks.

When Chloe got home, her mother was lying on the couch with her feet resting on a pillow.

"We're going to Chinatown next week!" said Chloe, handing her the permission slip.

"That sounds like fun," said her mother.

"Can you come?" said Chloe, resting her hand on Mrs. Kane's round stomach.

"I wish I could, honey, but the doctor wants me to keep off my feet for a while."

"Oh," said Chloe, patting her mother's stomach lightly. "Is the baby okay?"

"The baby is fine," said Mrs. Kane.

"I know!" said Chloe, rummaging in her knapsack and pulling out the orange. "This is for Michael," she said, holding it out to her mother.

"For Michael?" said Mrs. Kane, looking confused.

"You eat it, and he'll get it," said Chloe. "During the Chinese New Year, oranges stand for good luck."

Mrs. Kane took the orange and had started peeling it when there was a sound of running footsteps and a roaring noise, and Harry burst upon the scene.

"Harry!" said Chloe.

"What?" said Harry, stopping in his tracks.

Chloe couldn't resist, she just couldn't. *"Gung hay fat choy!"* shouted Chloe.

"Mommmm!" cried Harry, "Chloe's saying swear words."

"No, I'm not," said Chloe quickly. "It means happiness and good fortune."

"Terrific," said Mrs. Kane, and she ate the orange for good luck.

Chloe sat next to Mei-Hua on the bus ride to Chinatown. She felt special, because Mei-Hua knew almost as much about the Chinese New Year as her mother did.

"You and I were born in the Year of the Monkey," Mei-Hua told Chloe. "That means we're very funny, which we are. We're also very good at solving problems."

Chloe thought that Harry was much funnier. Her mother was always saying what a character he was. "Chloe's very responsible," she said about her eldest child. As for problem-solving, Chloe wondered if you had to be smart in math to do that, because math wasn't one of her best subjects.

Bucky interrupted her thoughts by calling from the seat behind her, "Look, everybody! A cemetery!"

Chloe knew that Harry would have loved the huge graveyard. The bus moved slowly through the traffic, so she could see lots of winged angels and huge crosses and statues, and rows and rows of tombstones, right in front of the city buildings.

"People are dying to get in!" said Bucky, laughing.

Chloe and Mei-Hua rolled their eyes at each other. Harry would have liked the joke, too.

At last they crossed the Williamsburg Bridge, and Mrs. Mellor told them they were nearly there. The bus swung left, and they drove past blocks of lighting stores.

"This is it," said Mei-Hua, and sure enough, the bus pulled to a stop.

Mrs. Mellor divided them into groups of five and put a grown-up in charge of each group. Chloe followed Mrs. Lee off the bus onto Pell Street, and they started walking.

They passed a fish store, but it didn't look like Mrs. Kane's fish store with its boring little slabs of white and orange fish lying all in a row. It was the most exciting fish store Chloe had ever seen. These fish had their heads on. Some of them were lying in icy water, their mouths opening and closing. Chloe had the feeling that if she leaned close enough they'd be saying, "Get me out of here!" Others were swimming around in large tanks. It was lucky for Chloe that Harry hadn't come, because he would have wanted to rescue the fish and take them home.

Bucky found a window full of cooked ducks and chickens, complete with heads, hanging all in a row. "Twelve of them!" he shouted.

Mrs. Lee told them that in many cultures the bird or fish was left complete, head and all, because completion meant perfection. The children crowded around the window and examined the hanging ducks.

"I hope we're not having chicken for lunch," whispered Ilana.

"It's not so bad," said Mei-Hua.

"Hot dogs are worse," said Chloe, hoping that Mei-Hua wasn't insulted. "They're made of pig's intestine."

Some of the children began a chicken count, up and down the narrow streets like Pell Street and Mott Street and Mulberry Street, until the total was one hundred and twenty-two ducks and chickens with their heads on.

Mei-Hua and Chloe counted pagodas, which were much prettier. There were three pagoda-covered phone booths, one pagoda-covered jewelry display, one pagoda-covered bank, and two pagoda-covered restaurants. Mrs. Lee showed them statues of the smiling Buddha, with his round belly, and the three Chinese gods that were in all the shop windows—the god of wealth, the god of good fortune, and the god of longevity.

At eleven-thirty they entered a Chinese restaurant all decorated in red. The tables had red tablecloths, and there was a fancy gold pagoda with a handsome god inside it on the main wall. Beneath him was an array of delicacies laid out on a flower-decorated table. Mrs. Lee pointed out the peanuts for long life, the coconut candy honoring parents, the kumquats for riches, and the candied ginger for smartness.

"That's me," said Bucky, reaching for the candied ginger. The restaurant owner let him taste one from another bowl.

Then they sat down at the red-covered tables and ate spring rolls and steaming bowls of wonton or hot-and-sour soup. Germaine and Tonya were brave and chose the spicy hot-and-sour soup. Germaine made believe steam was coming out of his ears when he ate it, but he scraped the bottom of the bowl. Then a waitress brought out two large platters with a mountain of fried rice on one and lo mein on the other.

"May I please have some duck sauce?" said Ilana.

Chloe put the bowl on the lazy Susan in the middle of the table, and Ilana took a spoonful.

"Do you realize where that duck sauce comes from?" said Bucky.

"Where?" said Ilana, a forkful of rice and duck sauce frozen halfway to her mouth.

"That's the gook that runs off the ducks hanging in the windows," said Bucky with a gleam in his eye.

"Sounds more like 'buck sauce' to me," said Germaine, hooting with laughter.

Ilana looked with alarm at Mrs. Lee, who shook her head.

"You know what I told you about doing good deeds during the Chinese New Year, Bucky," said Mrs. Lee. "Lying and bad behavior will get you into trouble."

Bucky's face turned pink, but it didn't stop him from grabbing the first fortune cookie when a plate of them was placed on the table, along with a dish of sliced oranges. Bucky cracked his cookie in two and popped one half into his mouth. Then he read the strip of paper. "Guard your worldly possessions" read the fortune.

"What's a worldly possession?" said Bucky.

"Your stuff," said Germaine. "Watch out that nobody messes with your stuff."

"Nobody's going to mess with my stuff," said Bucky. "Just let him try it!"

Mrs. Lee raised an eyebrow. "Good deeds, Bucky," she said.

Mei-Hua opened up her cookie and read, "You are one of the people who go places in life."

"Aren't you going to Disney World this summer?" said Chloe.

"You're right!" said Mei-Hua. "Now read yours, Chloe."

Chloe pulled out her white slip of paper and read, "You will come into some money." She crunched on her cookie. "Good," said Chloe between bites. "The only money I have is the three dollars spending money my mother gave me for this trip."

They ate slices of orange while Mrs. Mellor and Mrs. Lee paid for lunch. Bucky and Germaine wore their orange slices over their teeth so that they had orange-peel smiles. They leered at Chloe and Mei-Hua.

"My brother Harry does that all the time," said Chloe scornfully. That was when she noticed the dish holding three leftover fortune cookies—just enough to take home to Harry and Dorothy and Mei-Hua's sister, but not enough for Bucky's brother Ivan. While Bucky was busy making orange-slice smiles at Theresa, she sneaked them under the table. She tucked two of them away in her coat pocket and passed the third cookie to Mei-Hua. "For your sister," she

87

whispered. "I've got two for Dorothy and Harry." She would have to remember not to squash them.

After lunch they visited a statue of Confucius, the Chinese philosopher and teacher.

"Confucius believed in devotion to family," said Mrs. Lee, resting her hand on Mei-Hua's head. "And friends and ancestors, and peace and justice."

"He sounds like Martin Luther King," said Germaine. "He believed in peace and justice."

"They were both wise men," said Mrs. Lee, leading the way to a Buddhist temple. "Buddha was a real man also. His name was Siddhārtha Gautama, and he lived in India around 500 B.C. Now the Buddhists use the name for someone who embodies divine wisdom and virtue."

"Is it time for the gift store?" said Bucky.

Mrs. Lee looked at Mrs. Mellor, who nodded. "It's time," said Mrs. Lee, and she led them into a tiny store where three salespeople hovered close by as the children examined the fans and umbrellas, embroidered slippers and porcelain soup spoons, Chinese puzzles and calendars, dragon masks and ninja combat weapons. Chloe chose a fan that had beautiful flowers on it when she flipped it open, and Mei-Hua bought a pair of embroidered slippers. Bucky bought a Nunchuk before Mrs. Mellor had a chance to tell the class she would have no weapons on the bus, plastic or not. When they got outside, he waved it in the air until Mrs. Mellor said she would keep it for herself if he didn't put it in his pocket out of sight.

By the time they reached the bus and settled in their seats, the children were tired. Heads drooped and rested on their neighbors' shoulders, and the only noise was the sound of the bus's motor as they left Chinatown and drove across the bridge. Chloe held her fan in her lap and vowed to keep it away from Harry. Perhaps Dorothy could borrow it for dress-up, because she was more careful. Mei-Hua showed Chloe the pretty embroidery on her slippers.

They were just nodding off to sleep when from out of the blue, piercing the quiet, they heard a long wail. "My Nunchuk!" cried Bucky. "It's busted to bits!"

"See?" said Mei-Hua in Chloe's ear.

"What?" whispered Chloe.

"I guess he didn't watch out for his worldly possessions," said Mei-Hua.

Chloe patted her fan. It was in fine condition. She patted her coat pocket. Her fortune cookies were smashed to smithereens. Chloe had to laugh. "I didn't watch out for mine, either!" she said to Mei-Hua.

Bucky was quiet for the rest of the ride.

When Chloe got home, she kissed her mother hello, sniffed the air, and groaned.

"What's the matter?" said Mrs. Kane. "Didn't you enjoy Chinatown?"

"It was terrific," said Chloe, "but is that chicken I smell?"

"You love my honey-glazed chicken," said her mother, but when Chloe told her about the one hundred and twenty-two cooked ducks and chickens hanging with their heads on, she understood.

"You'll eat with me," said Mrs. Kane. "Ever since the day I thought I poisoned Grandpa and myself, I can't touch a bite of chicken."

Harry and Dorothy and Mr. Kane ate honey-glazed chicken and salad and baked potatoes in the kitchen. Chloe and her mother had crackers and grape jelly with glasses of milk on trays in the living room, just the two of them. Chloe told her mother all about Chinatown and the red-decorated restaurant and what Bucky said duck sauce was made of and Confucius and the smiling Buddha and the Year of the Dog and the Year of the Monkey and candied ginger for smartness and Bucky's broken Nunchuk and Chloe's broken cookies and her fortune.

"They leave the chicken head on for perfection," said Chloe, nibbling on a cracker. "You just have to get used to the idea."

"Maybe we'll take a family trip to Chinatown," said Mrs. Kane, "and you can show us everything."

"Harry would love the chickens," said Chloe, "but he'd try to take the fish home with him.

And Dorothy would love the pagodas and the smiling Buddha."

Mrs. Kane hugged Chloe. "The baby is very lucky to have a sister like you," she said.

Chloe leaned close to her mother's stomach. *"Gung hay fat choy!"* she said to the baby.

Then Chloe and her mother each had an orange for good luck.

6

Chloe's Fortune

CHLOE TOOK OUT her purple leather cowhide wallet, which Aunt Sarah had given her for her birthday. She had used it until all the birthday money that Grandpa and Grandma and her mother and father had given her was spent. Then it seemed silly to carry around an empty purse, even if it was such a pretty color.

Chloe was getting the wallet ready for her fortune, whenever she discovered it. She put her library card, ten Barbie stickers, and a Band-Aid with hearts on it in one of the plastic inserts.

"That's fake leather," said Harry. "Who ever

heard of a purple cow?" Then he flashed his snakeskin wallet and said, "Now this is real leather—genuine rattlesnake!" Pinned to the inside was his cowboy badge, and tucked in the billfold was a two-dollar bill. Harry pulled it out. "This lucky two-dollar bill has kept me lucky for a hundred years!" he said.

"That's pretty good for a first grader," said Chloe, putting the wallet on the couch while she fished in her pocket for her lucky fortune. She took the strip of paper and tucked it inside one of the clear plastic photo inserts so that she could see it every time she opened the wallet. The wallet was ready. Now all she needed was some money to put into it.

"Did you find any money yet?" said Dorothy, flopping down on the couch next to Chloe.

"Not yet," said Chloe. "But I will."

"Well, when you do, maybe you can buy me a present," said Dorothy, "because I'm such a great sister."

Harry squeezed next to Chloe on the other side. "And I'm a great brother," he said, bouncing up and down and singing, "great brother, great brother, great brother," until Chloe was ready to bop him over the head with her purple wallet. But she couldn't, because during the Chinese New Year you weren't supposed to fight or anything, and if she did, maybe she wouldn't find her fortune!

Chloe said, "You're squashing me," instead.

Harry jumped off the couch and held his face close to Chloe's. Then he pulled his lips back and made a weird kind of smile. "See my front tooth?" he said. "As soon as it falls out, I'll be richer than you, because the tooth fairy will come!"

"Big deal," said Chloe. "I have a box full of teeth in my dresser drawer."

"The sun is out," called Mrs. Kane, who had a Geiger counter in her head for fighting children. "Why don't you play outside?"

Harry ran and got his Superball while Chloe and Dorothy sat on the front steps.

"Now he's going to bounce that ball against the garage door," said Chloe, holding her head.

"When I get my fortune, I'm going to buy a room just for Harry to make noise in."

"Buy it soon," said Dorothy as Harry started hitting the door with such force that it shook.

"Is someone calling my name, or am I hearing things?" said Chloe.

"It's Mrs. Foster. She's waving for you to come over." Dorothy stood up and grabbed the ball from Harry. "Play catch with me," she said. "It's less noisy."

"I want to go with Chloe," said Harry.

Chloe felt like Maria, the crossing guard, as she rounded up Dorothy and Harry, looked both ways, and ushered them across the street.

"Hi, Mrs. Foster," said Chloe.

"You're just the person I want to see," said Mrs. Foster.

"Don't you want to see me?" said Harry.

"Of course," said Mrs. Foster. "But I have a job for Chloe because she's the oldest. I'll pay you twenty-five cents a day to take care of our goldfish while we're away."

"I knew it!" said Chloe.

"She knew it!" said Dorothy.

"We knew it!" said Harry.

"Oh, Mr. Foster told you already?" Mrs. Foster looked puzzled. "We only found out this morning that we were going."

"Where are you going?" said Harry nosily.

"Shush, Harry," said Chloe, in just the tone of voice her mother used when Harry was annoying her.

Mrs. Foster laughed. "We're going to visit my grandson Thomas in Boston. He's a few years younger than you, Harry."

"Has he lost any teeth yet?" said Harry. He made a terrible face so that Mrs. Foster could see his front tooth. "I can wiggle it," said Harry, demonstrating.

Mrs. Foster shuddered. "It looks like it's ready to come out," she said.

"When do I start?" said Chloe, changing the subject back to her job before Mrs. Foster got totally grossed out by Harry.

"Right now would be wonderful," said Mrs. Foster. "I'll go get Mr. Yellow and Mrs. Gold."

Harry bounced his Superball against the Foster's brick wall until the front door opened. Mrs. Foster walked like she was Great-Grandma Fanny in the nursing home, with tiny mincing little steps, down the stairs, carefully holding a small fish tank.

"Aren't you a little old for goldfish?" said Harry.

Mrs. Foster laughed again. "We keep them here for Thomas. He's crazy about them. He won them at the street fair the last time he was visiting, but he couldn't take them home on the plane with him."

Harry peered into the tank. "Which one is Mr. Yellow and which one is Mrs. Gold? They look the same."

"Mr. Yellow has a black speck on him," said Mrs. Foster, handing Chloe a jar of fish food. "Sprinkle some food in the tank once a day," she said. "And please don't overfeed them."

"My pet turtle Personality liked chopped meat," said Harry. "He died."

Mrs. Foster looked alarmed, until Chloe said

hastily, "I won't let him near the fish, Mrs. Foster. And I won't overfeed them."

"I'll carry them across the street for you," she said, "and make sure it's all right with your mother."

Mrs. Kane said it was fine, and Mrs. Gold and Mr. Yellow had a new home in Chloe's room for eight whole days, which to Chloe meant twenty-five cents times eight equals two whole dollars.

After Mrs. Foster left, Chloe made an announcement. "This is my first job, and it's my responsibility," she said. "I don't need anybody's help."

"I'll hand you the fish food," said Harry.

"I'll help you spend the money," said Dorothy.

"You'll both help me set the table for supper," said Mrs. Kane, shooing them into the kitchen.

Chloe looked at her watch. "It's five o'clock, Mrs. Gold and Mr. Yellow. Dinnertime." She turned the dial on the jar so that the little holes were showing, and sprinkled the little flakes on top of the water.

The fish just swam around. They didn't go near the food.

"Eat, Mrs. Gold. Eat, Mr. Yellow," Chloe crooned to the fish.

They continued to ignore their dinner. "Maybe you need some music," said Chloe. She thought for a minute, and then she sang "Five Little Ducks Went Swimming One Day," because she couldn't think of any fish songs, and at least they were swimming. The fish didn't touch their dinner. Then Chloe bent close to the tank. She was desperate, so she started singing, "Old MacDonald had a farm, E-I-E-I-O! And on that farm he had some fish, E-I-E-I-O!" Just as she sang "with a fish fish here, and a fish fish there," Mr. Yellow with the black spot swam to the surface and swallowed some food. Then Mrs. Gold followed.

"Good fish," said Chloe, relieved, and she hung a DO NOT DISTURB sign on her doorknob. Then she ran back into her room, wrote something on a piece of paper, put tape on the sides, and attached it to her sign. DO NOT DISTURB FISH, the sign read. Chloe sniffed. The fish were fed, and it smelled like her own supper was ready.

Harry obviously didn't believe in signs. He disappeared right after supper without even waiting for dessert, and Chloe found him in her room, bending over the fish tank. He wasn't singing to the fish. He was feeding them.

"What are you doing?" said Chloe, glaring at him.

"I gave them dessert!" said Harry, handing her the fish food.

"They don't eat dessert!" said Chloe, giving him a push out the door.

"I do," said Harry, and he headed back to the kitchen with Chloe following. Harry gulped like Mr. Yellow did. "Ice cream, ice cream," he said to his father.

"Frozen yogurt, frozen yogurt," said Mr. Kane, laughing as Harry made a face. "Is that tooth still hanging there?"

"He is so gross!" said Chloe, waiting for her father to give her a scoop. "And I caught him feeding my fish!"

"Harry, I warned you not to bother Chloe's fish. It's her job, you know."

Mr. Kane handed Harry a dish of raspberry frozen yogurt.

"Not this kind!" said Harry. "The seeds get caught in my teeth."

Mrs. Kane spooned some into her mouth. "It's better for me than ice cream," she said, patting her stomach.

"It's not better for me," said Harry, screwing up his nose.

"Raspberry's my favorite," said Chloe. "Anyway, maybe one of the seeds will knock out that disgusting tooth."

Harry brightened and ate a spoonful. "Nope," he said, wiggling his tooth with his tongue. "He doesn't want to leave me. I think he likes living in my mouth!"

"You're weird," said Chloe, and she picked up her dish of frozen yogurt and left the kitchen.

"Eat that on your desk," called Mrs. Kane, who was starting on her second scoop. "And if you spill any, wipe it up!"

Chloe opened her bedroom door with the DO NOT DISTURB FISH sign on the doorknob, and caught Dorothy in the act, sprinkling fish food into the tank.

"Stop!" said Chloe, banging her bowl of yogurt on the desk.

Dorothy jumped and dropped the fish-food container. It landed with a plop in Chloe's bowl of raspberry frozen yogurt.

"Now look what you did!" yelled Chloe, extracting the container as delicately as she could from the frozen yogurt. "It's all full of fish food!"

"You scared me!" said Dorothy, leaning over to examine the yogurt. "Maybe you can make believe it has chocolate bits sprinkled all over it," she said.

"No, thank you," said Chloe, clenching her teeth. She pointed to the door. *"Out!"*

"I never liked that kind anyway," said Dorothy. "The seeds get stuck in your teeth."

"Out out out!" shouted Chloe.

Chloe sat down. She took a piece of paper and wrote in huge letters THIS MEANS YOU! Then she taped it to the bottom of her DO NOT DISTURB FISH sign. She took her desk blotter, leaned it against the wall so that the fish tank was hidden, whispered, "Good night, Mr. Yellow and Mrs. Gold," turned out the light, got a favorite book to read, and got into bed. She would stay in her room and keep watch over Mrs. Gold and Mr. Yellow.

There was a knock on the door.

"What?" said Chloe, in a voice that did not invite anyone in.

"It's Harry," said Harry from outside the door.

"*So?*"

Harry opened the door an inch. "Dorothy told me about the frozen yogurt with the fish food in it."

"So?"

"I don't think it would taste good, either," said Harry.

"So?" Chloe's voice softened a little.

"So I brought you another bowl." Harry walked in, carrying the dish of frozen yogurt as carefully as Mrs. Foster had carried the fish tank.

"For you," said Harry, handing it to her.

"Sit here while I eat it," said Chloe, patting the bed.

Harry watched her in silence. Finally he said, "I won't tell Mom you're eating it in bed."

"Thanks," said Chloe, scraping the bottom of the bowl.

"Are you all finished?" said Harry.

"All finished," said Chloe. "It was delicious."

"Then we'd better brush our teeth," said Harry. "For the seeds."

Harry carried the empty bowl, and Chloe took the bowl of melted frozen yogurt and fish food, and they put them in the kitchen sink. Then they walked into the bathroom together. Harry took his blue toothbrush and squeezed some kid's toothpaste on it that tasted like bubble gum. Chloe took her red toothbrush and squeezed some minty grown-up toothpaste on it.

"Maybe my tooth will fall out when I brush," whispered Harry.

"Maybe," said Chloe, with a mouth full of toothpaste.

But it didn't.

Every evening at five o'clock for the next seven days, Chloe could be heard singing "Old Mac-

Donald Had a Farm" to Mr. Yellow and Mrs. Gold.

"The concert's beginning," Dorothy would yell.

"I hear something fishy!" was Harry's big joke.

Mrs. Kane tried to teach Chloe another fish song called "When the Boat Comes In," because it had a fishie in it, and a haddock, too. "It's so much prettier," she told Chloe. But Chloe refused. She said that only "with a fish fish here, and a fish fish there" worked.

On Saturday, Grandma and Grandpa came to supper. Mrs. Kane made spaghetti with turkey meatballs instead of honey-glazed chicken, just in case Chloe wasn't ready for chicken yet.

"I hear you have a job," Grandpa said to Chloe.

"By tomorrow morning, I've earned two dollars," Chloe said proudly.

"By tomorrow morning, maybe my tooth will fall out," said Harry, "and I'll be rich like Chloe."

"Why don't we just tie a string around it and attach it to Dad's fender," said Dorothy, "like they do it in the cartoons?"

"That sounds gruesome!" said Mrs. Kane, patting her round stomach.

"You look tired, honey," said Grandma Rebecca, rubbing Chloe's mother's cheek like she was a little girl.

"I'm exhausted," said Mrs. Kane. "I'm going to bed early tonight."

Grandpa pushed himself back from the table. "Let's clear our plates and go see those fish of yours," he said.

They went upstairs to Chloe's room.

"Mr. Yellow especially likes the sun," explained Chloe, "so I leave my desk lamp on for him until bedtime."

Chloe leaned over the tank. "What's that?" she shrieked, pointing to a green body floating on top of the water.

"That's my deep-sea fisherman," explained Harry. "He's going fishing."

"Not for my fish, he's not," said Chloe, scooping him out of the tank.

"Fish get bored, too," said Harry. "He was keeping them company."

"They're not bored," said Chloe hotly. "I sing

to them all the time, and I talk to them, too."

Harry shrugged his shoulders and turned to Grandpa Leon. "Wouldn't you like some company if you were a fish?" he said.

"It seems to me, Harry," said Grandpa, "that these two have each other."

"Like you and Grandma?" said Harry.

"Just like that," he said.

Chloe hugged Grandpa Leon. "You're the best grandpa," she told him. "I have to get something for you."

She grabbed a marker from her desk and ran downstairs. On the refrigerator door was Chloe's picture of Mrs. Gold and Mr. Yellow, decorated with little red hearts. Across the top of it, Chloe wrote, "For the best grandpa in the world."

Then she ran upstairs to her room. Inside, bending over the fish tank, was the best grandpa in the world. He was feeding the fish.

"Grandpa!" said Chloe.

"They looked hungry," said Grandpa meekly.

Chloe handed Grandpa the picture. "It's for you," she said.

He took the picture and kissed Chloe on top of the head. "I'd better find Grandma," he mumbled.

Chloe peered into the tank. She scooped four marbles out of the bottom of the bowl that she hadn't seen before. Thank goodness tomorrow she could say good-bye to Mr. Yellow and Mrs. Gold. Thank goodness they were still alive and swimming.

On Sunday, Mrs. Foster took the goldfish back to her house and gave Chloe two dollars. Chloe tucked the money into her purple cowhide wallet and caught a glimpse of her fortune. "You will come into some money," it said. It never told her she would have to earn it, or that it would be such hard work, on account of her very helpful family that thought they knew so much about fish.

That night, Chloe settled into bed. She looked at the wallet on her desk, in the very spot where the fishbowl had been. The two dollars meant much more to her than the birthday money

Grandma and Grandpa had given her. She decided she would look for another job to earn some more money. It was hard to sleep, and she took her flashlight off the shelf so that she could read without her mother noticing.

"The baby was kicking like crazy last night," Chloe could hear her mother saying in the hallway. "I hope I can get some sleep tonight." Mr. Kane mumbled something, and the door to their bedroom closed. The house was quiet, and Chloe read.

She was just ready to go to sleep when she heard a noise. Chloe strained her ears to listen. It was someone crying.

It was Harry. Chloe got out of bed and walked over to her parents' bedroom door. "Harry's crying," she whispered. No one answered. Chloe pressed her ear to the door. She heard snoring.

Harry was crying more noisily now. Chloe went into his bedroom and sat on the bed. "What's the matter, Harry?" she said. "Are you sick?"

"Yes," said Harry, only it sounded like "yeth."

"I'm sick because my front tooth is missing," he said.

"It fell out!" said Chloe. "But isn't that what you've been waiting for?"

"It's lost!" wailed Harry. "It's gone! I can't find it anywhere, and now the tooth fairy won't find it and she won't give me any money for it."

Chloe looked at her little brother, the same little brother who floated a deep-sea fisherman in her fish tank, and who once pulled the head off her favorite Barbie doll. The same little brother who thought she was as smart as an eagle, and who brought her a bowl of frozen yogurt because he knew she wouldn't like fish food in it. His eyes were red and his round cheeks were wet and his covers were scrunched up to his chin.

"The tooth fairy has very special powers," whispered Chloe.

Harry hiccuped. "Are you sure?" he whispered, before another sob erupted.

"Wait and see," said Chloe. She kissed him on his round wet cheek and he closed his eyes.

She went back to her room and found an envelope. Disguising her handwriting, she wrote *From the tooth fairy* across it. Then she found a small white box in the top drawer of her dresser, removed an object from it, and carefully placed it in the envelope. Finally she took the two dollars she'd earned from feeding Mr. Yellow and Mrs. Gold, put them in the envelope, and sealed it.

The next morning, Chloe and Dorothy were helping their mother make breakfast when they heard Harry screaming so loudly that Mrs. Kane dropped a frozen waffle on the floor.

"What on earth is he saying?" Mrs. Kane said to Mr. Kane, who was putting milk in his coffee.

"Something's too hairy," said Mr. Kane, straining his ears to listen.

Harry burst into the room. "The tooth fairy!" he screamed. "The tooth fairy came!"

Mrs. Kane put her hand to her mouth. Mr. Kane froze, holding his coffee cup in midair.

"She came!" cried Harry.

"She did?" said Mrs. Kane.

"She did?" said Mr. Kane.

"I lost my tooth, and she found it for me, and

she gave me two whole dollars and my tooth to keep!" said Harry breathlessly.

"Can I see it?" said Mrs. Kane.

Harry handed her the envelope. She read, "From the tooth fairy," and removed a small yellow tooth from inside. "It was nice of the tooth fairy to leave you the tooth," said Mrs. Kane.

"I'm going to put it in my pencil case," said Harry, grabbing the tooth and running out of the room.

"Which one of you did it?" whispered Mrs. Kane.

"Not me," said Dorothy. "Maybe it was really the tooth fairy!"

"You were sound asleep," said Chloe. "And I heard him crying, so I gave him one of my old baby teeth."

Mrs. Kane hugged her. "All your hard-earned money," she whispered.

"I couldn't find my front tooth," said Chloe, "but I don't think he noticed the difference."

"I don't think so, either," said Mr. Kane. "We're very proud of you, honey."

Mrs. Kane peered around the corner to see if

Harry was coming. She took two dollars out of her purse and slipped them into Chloe's pocket. "Take it, honey. You helped us so much by being Harry's tooth fairy. We don't want you to spend your own money."

Before Chloe could say a word, Harry arrived. "I'm starved!" he said. "Where's my waffle?"

"Chloe gets the first one," said Mrs. Kane. She put a golden brown waffle in front of her oldest child, with a scoop of raspberry frozen yogurt on top. Then she put plain waffles, with syrup on top, in front of Harry and Dorothy.

"No fair!" said Harry. "How come I don't get one like that?"

"You don't like the seeds," said Chloe, flashing him a big smile.

"Oh," said Harry. "I forgot." Then he flashed his sister a big gap-toothed smile back.

7

Mickey

WHEN HARRY FOUND OUT that the baby was going to be a boy, he shouted, "Hurray!"

Mr. Kane winked at Chloe. "How about naming the baby Dakota?" he said to Harry.

Harry made a face. "Isn't that a state?" he said. "Why don't we call him New Jersey instead?"

Mr. Kane laughed. "Chloe thinks the baby should be called Michael," he said.

"He looks like a Michael," said Chloe.

"Maybe he looks like a Harry," said Harry. "Maybe we should call him Harry the Second."

"I think he'd like his own name," said Mrs. Kane. "What do you think, Dorothy?"

Dorothy bent over her mother's tummy. "What do you think, little baby?" she said.

"Burp!" said Harry. "He wants to be called Burp."

Harry continued to call the baby Burp on the way to Walnut School, until his best friend Benjamin joined him. Then they tried to out-burp each other.

Dorothy rolled her eyes. "Boys are disgusting, aren't they?" she said to Chloe.

"And just think," said Chloe. "In a little while, we're going to have two of them in the house!"

They stood next to Maria, the crossing guard, and waited for her signal that they could step into the street.

"How's your mom doing?" she said to Chloe, an arm in front of Harry and Benjamin.

"She's getting big!" said Chloe.

"She looks like my basketball," said Harry, leaning into Maria's arm.

"You're a real pip, Harry," said Maria. "You remind me of my son when he was little."

116

"You tell me that every time you see me!" said Harry, walking backward alongside her.

"You're just like him," said Maria, turning him around. "Eyes in front of you in the street, young man," she said as Harry stepped up onto the sidewalk and ran like a jackrabbit into the school yard. Maria watched him and started laughing so loudly that Chloe thought she saw some birds fly out of a nearby tree.

"Was he fresh like Harry?" said Chloe.

"Fresh as baked bread," said Maria, "and smart as a whip."

"Harry wants to call the baby Harry the Second," said Chloe.

"Or Burp," said Dorothy.

"He's a pip!" said Maria, waving good-bye to Chloe and Dorothy.

They waved back. Then Dorothy whispered to Chloe, "What's a pip?"

"Mom says Harry is a real character," said Chloe, looking for Mei-Hua in the school yard. "She usually says it after he does something funny. I think a pip is like that."

117

"So I guess it's good," said Dorothy, waving to her best friend Jessica.

"I think so," said Chloe. "Remember when he wouldn't take his cowboy hat off, even in the bathtub?"

"Or when he was sleeping," said Dorothy.

"That must be a pip," said Chloe, just as the first bell rang.

When school was over, Maria was waiting for them at the crosswalk as usual. "It's getting colder," she said to the children. "Put on your hood, Harry." Maria bent over Harry and wrapped his scarf more snugly around him. Then she herded them across the street.

When they were safely on the sidewalk, Maria pulled a photograph out of her pocket. "Look," said Maria. "Doesn't my son Michael look like Harry?"

Chloe examined the picture. "He has Harry's eyes," she said.

"And his round face," said Dorothy, peering over her shoulder.

Harry grabbed the picture. "He looks smart like me, Maria," he said.

118

"He's an accountant now," said Maria, smiling. She took the photograph, wiped it gently on her coat, and put it back in her pocket.

"That's so smart I don't know what it is!" said Harry, waving to his mother as she came out of the house to watch for them.

Mrs. Kane gave them a snack in the kitchen.

"How many years has Maria been a crossing guard?" said Chloe, munching on a chocolate chip cookie.

"Oh, ages," said Mrs. Kane. "Since her kids were little." She gazed at the carrot in her hand. "Now why does your cookie look so much better than my carrot?"

"Because it is," said Harry.

Chloe handed her mother a cookie. "Just have one," she said. "Maria says Harry is a real pip."

"She's crazy about me," said Harry. "She says I'm just like her son Michael."

"Michael was her first," said Mrs. Kane, taking a big bite of her cookie. "Some people have a soft spot for their first babies."

"Really?" said Chloe happily.

119

"But you don't, do you?" said Dorothy, the middle child.

Mrs. Kane laughed. "I have a soft spot for each one of you," she said, reaching for a second cookie.

"You have a soft spot for cookies," said Chloe.

"Does that mean the baby will like chocolate chip cookies, too?" said Dorothy, dunking hers in milk like a doughnut.

"Maybe the baby will have chocolate chip spots all over his face," said Harry, crowing.

His mother laughed. "Maybe he'll have your imagination, Harry. Actually, I ate a lot of ice cream when I was pregnant with you," said Mrs. Kane, "and that's your favorite, isn't it?"

"What did you eat when you were pregnant with me?" said Chloe.

"Lots of fish," said Mrs. Kane, "because I heard it was good for the brain."

"Oh, gross!" said Chloe. "How disgusting!"

"I told you that you're just like an eagle," said Harry. "Eagles like fish, and they're the smartest birds in the world."

Mrs. Kane put the cookies away. "I don't remember what I ate when I was pregnant with Dorothy," she said. "I was so exhausted that as soon as Chloe went to sleep, I got into bed and watched movies."

"Maybe that's why I want to be an actress!" said Dorothy.

"I'm going to be a postman," said Harry, "except I'm going to wear roller skates to speed up the delivery."

"How about speeding into your room and doing your homework?" said Mrs. Kane.

Harry jumped up from the table and ran out of the kitchen.

He was back before Mrs. Kane had a chance to say another word.

"You're in luck, Mom," said Harry, out of breath.

"Why is that, dear?" said Mrs. Kane.

"Because tomorrow in cooking class, we're making chocolate chip cookies," said Harry, "and we can continue the experiment."

"What experiment is that?" said his mother.

"To see if the baby comes out with chocolate

chip spots!" announced Harry, and he was gone.

Mrs. Kane looked at Chloe and rolled her eyes.

"Maria is right," said Chloe. "Harry is a real pip."

"You can say that again," said her mother.

Chloe and Dorothy and Harry all took cooking class after school on Thursdays. Chloe and Mei-Hua entered the cafeteria and took their places behind a long table where the fourth graders sat. She could see Dorothy at the next table, but Harry was on the other side of the room.

Chloe sniffed. "Peeww!" she said to her best friend Mei-Hua. "This place smells like old hot dogs and mustard!"

Mrs. Erickson put out a sack of flour, brown sugar, eggs, vanilla, baking soda, and some spoons and measuring cups. She winked at Chloe. "Soon we'll have this place smelling of chocolate!" she said. She poured some chocolate chips into paper cups and gave every pair of bakers some chips and a sheet of paper with the recipe on it. "If I catch anyone eating these chocoate chips," she said firmly, "he or she will be cleaning up instead of baking."

Chloe glanced at the recipe. Being the best angel food cake baker in the world, she knew that her cookies would be exceptional. She knew that Dorothy's cookies would be sensational. But Harry's? Her brother could hardly read yet. She squinted her eyes to see who his partner was, and her heart sank. It was Bucky Seeger's younger brother Ivan, who was even more of a wiseguy than Bucky.

Chloe raised her hand. "I don't think my brother Harry can follow this recipe," she explained to Mrs. Erickson.

"I don't, either," said Mrs. Erickson, laughing. "So I gave the first graders some ready-made dough for them to mix in the chocolate chips and then make into their own cookie shapes."

Chloe and Mei-Hua got busy. They took turns creaming the butter, and then they added the sugar, egg, and vanilla.

"Oh, dear," said Mei-Hua in a loud voice. "I got cookie dough on my finger!"

"Me, too!" said Chloe, and she and Mei-Hua laughed and licked their fingers clean. Chloe consulted her recipe. "Now we add the flour," she said.

"And the salt and the baking soda," said Mei-Hua, carefully measuring half-teaspoons of each.

Then they mixed and mixed until the batter was smooth and ready to be spooned onto a cookie sheet.

"Finished!" said Chloe, wiping her hands on a paper towel.

Mei-Hua waved her hand excitedly. "We're finished, Mrs. Erickson," she said. "They can go into the oven!"

Mrs. Erickson looked at the cookie sheet. "Very good," she said. "I see you remembered to grease the pan. I see you left plenty of room around each cookie. There's only one thing you forgot."

"What?" said Chloe, looking blankly at Mrs. Erickson. She had a reputation to maintain, being the best angel food cake baker in the world.

"The chocolate chips!" said Mrs. Erickson, smiling widely. "Unless, of course, you plan on leaving them out!"

Chloe clapped her hand to her mouth. "Never!" she said.

"No way!" said Mei-Hua.

"Then you'd better get busy," said Mrs. Erickson, consulting her watch as she walked away.

"Do we have to squash all the cookies back into the bowl?" said Mei-Hua, sighing.

"Not if I can help it," said Chloe, taking a handful of chocolate chips. Cookie by cookie, Chloe sprinkled some chips on top. Then she pushed them down so that they were embedded in the cookie dough. "And I was worried about Harry," she whispered to Mei-Hua, who was busy pushing chocolate chips into her row of cookies.

At last they finished, and Mrs. Erickson took the tray from them. Chloe looked over at Dorothy, who was already eating one of her cookies. She craned her neck to check out Harry. Harry was sitting down with his head in his hands, and a lady was bending over him. Then the lady walked toward Chloe.

"I think you're needed over here," she said. "Your brother seems to be having some kind of problem."

"I'll bet it has something to do with Bucky Seeger's little brother," said Chloe, following the lady.

"Do you think so?" said the lady. "I'm Mrs. Seeger and that's my son Ivan. I asked him, but he says he doesn't know."

Chloe could feel her face burning as she leaned down over her little brother. "What's the matter, Harry?" she said.

Harry looked up at her. His face was tear-streaked and there were dried patches of cookie dough on his cheeks. "Look," he said, pointing to a cookie shaped into a lopsided cowboy hat. A tear slid down his face.

"I've told him it's a lovely cookie," said Ivan Seeger's mother. "He won't stop crying."

"He hit me," piped up Ivan.

"I know, dear," said his mother, resting a hand on his head.

126

"I did not!" said Harry, his lip trembling.

"I'd like to talk to him alone, please," said Chloe.

"Go ahead," said Mrs. Seeger, pulling Ivan away from Harry.

Chloe looked at her brother. He was a pip. He was a character. He had a strange and vivid imagination. But he wasn't a troublemaker.

"You can tell me, Harry," Chloe whispered into his ear.

Harry shook his head. "She won't believe me," he whispered back.

"She won't believe you?" said Chloe.

"The sugar," said Harry, a tear sliding down his face and landing on the lopsided cookie. "Ivan said our dough needed sugar even though his mother said it was already mixed, and he gave me a cup of it and I poured it in," said Harry, his lower lip quivering.

"So?" said Chloe, stroking his hair. "It'll be sweeter than the rest, that's all."

"T—t—t—taste it," said Harry, pulling off a piece of hat brim and handing it to her.

Chloe popped it in her mouth and chewed.

"Eeeeeew!" she said, looking around for a place to spit it out.

"Here," said Harry, handing her a paper towel. "It's salty, isn't it?"

"It's gross!" said Chloe.

"I told her it was too salty," said Harry, "but she wouldn't believe me."

"Did she taste it?" said Dorothy.

"No," said Harry.

Chloe picked up the lopsided cowboy hat cookie and marched over to Mrs. Seeger, who was helping little Ivan put his coat on.

"Taste this," she said, breaking off a piece.

"No, thank you, honey, I'm on a diet," said Mrs. Seeger, tying the strings of Ivan's hood under his chin.

"My brother doesn't lie," said Chloe.

Mrs. Seeger raised her eyebrows. "I didn't say he was lying," she said to Chloe. "I told him he was imagining things."

"What's going on here?" said Mrs. Erickson.

"Taste my brother's cookie," said Chloe to Mrs. Erickson.

Mrs. Erickson wasn't on a diet, and she nibbled on a piece until her mouth stopped chewing and she made a terrible, horrible face. "Are they all like this?" she said to Mrs. Seeger. "It's awful!"

Mrs. Seeger bent down and untied little Ivan's hood. She pulled the hood off his head. "What did you do to the cookie dough?" she said between her teeth.

"Salt," peeped Ivan. "I added salt."

"I told her," said Harry. "I really did."

Mrs. Seeger turned to Harry. "I owe you an apology," she said. Chloe thought she looked more mad than sorry. Then Mrs. Seeger turned toward Ivan. "Apologize to Harry," she said sharply.

"It was only a joke," said Ivan.

"Then why didn't you put salt in your own cookie dough?" said Harry.

Ivan shrugged, and before he could say any more, Mrs. Seeger was pulling him out of the cafeteria. Chloe noticed that she didn't even put his hood back on.

Mei-Hua came over with a paper plate full of cookies. "I divided ours into three," she said, "so Harry could have some."

"Thanks," said Harry, biting into one. "It tastes good without salt." Harry smiled up at Chloe, his face round and sweet-looking. It was not the face of a little boy who once pulled the head off her favorite Barbie doll. "You're the best sister in the world," said Harry.

On Friday morning, Chloe noticed that something was not right at the crosswalk. From a distance, Maria was shorter and thinner and very serious looking. Up close, Maria was not Maria.

"Who are you?" said Harry to the strange crossing guard.

"I'm Carla," said the lady. She didn't put her hand in front of Harry like Maria did. She didn't even smile.

"Where's Maria?" said Chloe, following Carla across the street.

"She has family problems," said Carla.

Maria had family problems after school, too.

Carla walked them across the street without even saying hello. When Harry and Benjamin made fish faces, Carla didn't laugh. She didn't say a word.

"Maria has family problems," announced Harry as they walked into the kitchen.

"I know," said Mrs. Kane. "I saw her husband."

"What's the matter?" said Chloe.

"Her son was in a car accident," said Mrs. Kane. "She's with him at the hospital."

"Michael?" said Harry. "The one like me?"

"The one like you," said Mrs. Kane. "Mr. Cassio said his seat belt saved him."

Harry munched on a cheese stick. "He was smart to buckle up," he said.

"Maria must be upset," said Chloe. "Is there anything we can do?"

"Not really," said Mrs. Kane, putting a plate of sliced apple on the table.

"We'll make some cookies!" said Chloe. "And a card!" She consulted her mother, and they took a bowl and some sugar and butter and flour and vanilla and baking soda out of the closet. They preheated the oven. Chloe measured, and Harry and Dorothy mixed. Chloe spooned some of the mixture in even mounds on the cookie sheet, ready for baking. It was much faster the second time around.

While Harry and Dorothy made a card, Chloe sat down to write a poem.

Dear Maria, she wrote. It wasn't easy. In fact, it was almost as hard as Grandma's poem, because nothing rhymed with crosswalk, and nothing rhymed with cookies, and nothing at all rhymed with Michael.

Chloe called to her mother. "Can you think of anything that rhymes with Michael?"

Mrs. Kane stood in the doorway. "Recycle?" she said.

"It's not a poem about the environment," said Chloe. Motorcycle would never do, especially since he was in a car accident. Chloe put down her pencil and sighed.

"You'll think of something," said Mrs. Kane. "You always do."

Chloe picked up her pencil again. She had an idea. She wrote down a line and erased it. She scribbled and scratched out and wrote some more. At last the poem was finished, and Harry and Dorothy and Mrs. Kane gathered in the living room for her to read it.

Chloe stood in front of her mother's favorite potted tree. She wasn't an actress like Dorothy or a clown like Harry. She cleared her throat and read the poem out loud.

"*We're sending you this little letter,*
  in the hopes that your son is all better.
  Harry says life is sad,
  crossing streets is so bad.
  (The new lady didn't smile when we met her.)

"*So we hope that these cookies aren't sticky,*
  Or gooey or gluey or icky.
  With our love they've been sent,
  or they'll make good cement,
  but we'd rather you gave them to Mickey."

Harry was miffed. "My cookies don't taste like cement," he said.

"It's a joke," said Chloe.

"How come you called him Mickey?" said Dorothy.

"Because nothing rhymes with Michael," said Chloe. "I thought it was a good idea at the time." Chloe read the poem to herself. "Maybe you're right," she said doubtfully. "Maybe Maria won't know who Mickey is."

Dorothy took the poem from her sister. "It's great," she said.

"It's better than I could ever do," said Harry, watching as Dorothy taped the poem into the card he'd helped make. "But I still say my cookies don't taste like cement."

"You've lost your sense of humor, Harry," said Chloe, happy again. "I was born in the Year of the Monkey, and we have the ability to make people laugh."

Harry laughed. Then each of them signed the card, and Mrs. Kane put it on the shelf in the hallway, beside the box of cookies she had packed.

"If she's not there in the morning," said Mrs.

Kane, "we'll drop it off at her house after school."

After breakfast, Chloe and Dorothy and Harry didn't dawdle. They were hoping that Maria would be at the crosswalk. Harry ran out the front door and Chloe and Dorothy and Mrs. Kane followed.

"It feels like spring is on the way," said Mrs. Kane, taking a deep breath.

"We can start looking for crocuses," said Chloe, checking the front yard. She stopped when she heard sounds of laughter at the crosswalk. Maria's laughter.

"She's there!" said Chloe, running with the card and the cookies.

Maria had her arm around Harry as Chloe and Dorothy handed her the present.

"It's for Michael," said Chloe.

"The cookies don't taste like cement," said Harry.

Maria opened the card and read it. Chloe could see tears spring into the corners of her eyes.

"It's beautiful," said Maria, wiping her eyes

135

with a gloved hand. "How did you know that I've called my son Mickey since he was a baby?"

"Nothing rhymed with Michael," said Chloe, grinning.

Mrs. Kane put an arm around her oldest daughter. "Chloe can solve any problem," she said proudly.

"I'm good at it," explained Chloe. "I was born in the Year of the Monkey."

Chloe looked at her mother's smiling face. She looked down at her mother's tummy. Harry was absolutely right. Her stomach did look like a basketball. Chloe patted the roundness, the baby brother that she couldn't wait to see, and she remembered her angry composition about being the oldest. If she had to write it all over again, she would change it. Harry the pip was right for the second time. Chloe *was* the best sister in the world, except for Dorothy. And when Michael was born, she would show him just how terrific she was. She could even call him Mickey if she wanted to. After all, nothing whatsoever rhymed with Michael.